VAMPEIRE: THE DEBUTANTE

VAMPEIRE:
THE DEBUTANTE

Andrea White

Book Guild Publishing
Sussex, England

First published in Great Britain in 2011 by
The Book Guild Ltd
Pavilion View
19 New Road
Brighton, BN1 1UF

Typesetting in Baskerville by
Nat-Type, Cheshire

Printed and bound by CPI Group (UK) Ltd, Croydon, CR0 4YY

A catalogue record for this book is available from
The British Library.

ISBN 978 1 84624 623 4

Prologue

The vampire's head hung low, his mind filtering images of his distraught wife and their life together. The vamp he despised stood before him, and he knew the Council's deliberations were only a formality. His crime carried a predetermined sentence: escape was an unforgivable violation of the rules, but taking a wife was even worse. He would suffer at the vamp's hand. Extinction alone would never be enough for her.

The pursuit commenced with a hundred-metre sprint through a tunnel of trees, though he was given an initial advantage. Then the four femme fatales gave chase. Other vamps hovered round in an invisible coliseum while the vampires – their captive mates – stood behind them, pale and cowed. His wife was flanked by two vamps. They were all forced to witness the vamps stalking closer, and closer, and closer.

Vamps watched in fervour; some watched in disgust. The vampires and his wife … in anguish!

They outnumbered, outsmarted and outmanoeuvred him as the distance between them decreased. Their stalking mirrored the hunting patterns of lionesses, but even an entire pride of lions could not have eluded these savage beasts.

A fraction of a second and they pounced. They trapped and then threw him from side to side with a force that shattered even his stony-hard frame. Their harsh jaws savaged his ashen hide. His attempts to struggle were futile; they held him firmly and tore him limb from limb. In the end he was nothing but a pile of mangled flesh.

Briege intended that every vampire present should store this retribution in their memories. Those shrill screams would ring in their ears for ever; they would remember suffering each blow with him!

Once more thunderous roars echoed through the coliseum as the Council undertook its final act and ritual – incineration, to ensure his utter extinction and scatter his ashes on foreign shores.

1

Layla

Layla opened her curtains and looked at the grey, cloudy horizon. She sat on her bed and crumpled her duvet in her delicate, pale hand. She shivered, remembering the cold of the early hours.

Ironic, she thought.

She made her bed; her pillow was saturated. In a daze she remembered her dream. She put the pillow to her cheek and felt the dampness. It was a recurrent dream. She'd been dreaming it since they arrived in Glasgow, and remembered how it had coincided with her mother taking ill.

They had moved to Glasgow to live with her mother's sister, Kate. Layla enrolled in a local school and even managed to find a part-time job. Her mother had been ill for almost four years. Strangely, it had been the longest and most settled period of Layla's seventeen years.

Layla had been uprooted so many times. When her mother decided it was time to move on from one place to another, a new 'adventure' ensued. They'd lived throughout various parts of South Africa, Belgium, France and England. Finally, they had arrived in Glasgow, Scotland. Her mum used to say they'd been bitten by the travel bug and their fate lay in its hands.

As Layla fluffed her duvet, folded it neatly along the seam

of the pillow, she raised her head and stared out the window. She puzzled over the 'travel bug': perhaps it had given her mother the disease that seemed to be draining the very life from her in front of her eyes.

Layla shook her head and her chain of thought quickly changed; the dream entered her mind again. She noticed how it never faltered. The lone figure glistened, remaining motionless and staring at her with gemstone eyes. At times the eyes were vacant; at other times they danced, shiny and bright. There were plants either side of the form. On the left was a white rosebush and on the right was a solo sycamore tree. Layla could make out every tiny detail of each leaf and bud. The figure seemed vaguely familiar to her, but it always faded away before she had time to recognise it.

The clang and clutter of cutlery and crockery snapped Layla from her daydream. She flew downstairs, through the living room and stood in the doorway of the large kitchen. She knew even before she saw her that her aunt was the one clanking about with the dishes; it was always her. Although each time Layla heard the noise, she wished it was her mother.

'Morning Layla,' Aunt Kate said, before turning round to face her.

Layla had given up being surprised by her aunt's ability to sense her.

'Morning,' she whispered, and then paused.

Aunt Kate was standing in silence, waiting for her to speak. She didn't want to put Layla under too much pressure.

'Is Mum sleeping?' she eventually asked.

Kate turned to face her. Her lips creased with a smile as she handed Layla a large, strong coffee. Layla returned her smile.

'Happy birthday, Layla!'

'Thanks,' Layla replied.

'I thought you might sleep longer this morning, you must be exhausted,' she stated.

Layla leaned forward and pecked her aunt on the cheek as she flinched. She'd forgotten how little her aunt enjoyed affection and she usually assumed it had something to do with her not having children of her own. It was odd, though. Her aunt often seemed cold, which was quite the opposite of her mother.

'The coffee's lovely and warm,' Layla said. She shivered. 'I wasn't really very tired.'

'I've noticed,' Kate remarked.

'Is the doctor coming out today?' Layla asked, trying to avoid her aunt's gaze.

'Yes,' Kate said, 'and a nurse too.' She paused. 'Layla,' she said, 'you do know she is deteriorating quite rapidly?'

Layla nodded. The pain was written all over her face. Her heart ached in her chest. Kate looked a little squeamish.

'Do you want to see if she's awake? I'm sure she'll want to see you,' Kate said.

She ushered Layla away toward her mother's room. At first Layla was reluctant, but then, with a sudden enthusiastic burst, she ran. As they reached Layla's mother's room, Kate pursed her lips anxiously.

Layla crossed the threshold of the door and watched the slight rise and fall of her mother's chest. She counted the shallow breaths and noted how her mother's slight frame looked almost to be shrinking. Fresh lines seemed to have appeared overnight, covering her pale face. Layla could never accept that Marie might have given up and yet her mother was disappearing before her. Layla wanted a cure. She wanted her mother back; back to the person she knew before.

'Hi, Mummy,' she whispered, kneeling beside the bed.

Layla placed her mother's hand in hers and pushed it gently against her cheek. A sudden, but weak jerk, and Marie drew her hand away.

'You're cold,' she muttered.

'I know,' Layla replied, 'I've turned the heating on. It's this Scottish weather. I can't acclimatise at all.'

Layla giggled. Her mother forced her mouth to curl, acknowledging her funny sense of humour. Layla's eyes burned; she felt the need to alleviate the permanent lump in her throat, but she was unable to let go. She was grateful in some way; it saved her mother any further pain.

'Happy birthday,' Marie whispered as she choked, breathless.

'Thanks, Mum,' Layla said and then gently kissed her forehead.

Marie was attempting to point. She was so weak, but her eyes lingered on the bedside cabinet and Layla knew she wanted her to open the drawer. Inside the drawer lay an envelope and a gift wrapped in pretty pink paper. She recognised the writing; her mother must have written it when she was more able. Layla smiled. Marie drifted in and out of consciousness. Layla leaned over her once again and kissed her cheek. She didn't mean to wake her, but Marie opened her eyes.

'Thank you,' Layla whispered.

'Open it,' Marie managed.

Layla opened the gift trying not to tear the paper. Layla giggled; she remembered her mother shouting for her to hurry up and rip the paper as a way of exciting her when she was a little girl.

It was a small green-velvet box and inside was a beautiful white-gold pendant, suspended from a matching chain. The pendant, an antique trinket, had what seemed like two interlocking *E*s and an emerald nestled between them. There were four small diamonds at the tip of each triangle; they twinkled in the light. A perfect gift, Layla thought, a true memento of her mother.

Marie saw that Layla understood how deeply meaningful the gift was. Layla caressed her arm, acknowledging how grateful she was. She opened the card and a large wad of banknotes fell to the floor. She leaned over to pick them up. Her mother had never been wealthy and now she knew why; it must have been her entire life savings. Layla felt an immediate pang of guilt; she did not need the money. She had given her something more than any amount of money. Layla thought of her aunt's contrasting and endless wealth. Money was no object for her and she was most generous with it. It seemed of no value to her at all. But even Kate's wealth could not buy the one thing she wanted most, her mother's health. Layla would have given every penny and more for her mother to be well.

'Mum!'

Marie did not acknowledge her cry. Everything she had to say was written in the card. Layla smiled; she knew exactly what her silence meant.

The birthday card said little more than the usual endearments but between the folded halves was also a sealed envelope. Layla opened it and read her mother's letter:

To my dearest Layla,
Seventeen years of joy – where have they gone?
I know you will be the most wonderful adult; you've never really been a child …

Layla stopped reading; she had no tears but inside her heart was crying out.

She read on:

… You have spirit, intelligence and beauty, and you have brought me nothing but joy. I love you and you know that. I cannot offer you any advice except that you should be happy in all you do. Remember; a life with love is a fulfilling one. I hope you experience it as much as I have. I will take your love, and your father's with me, wherever I go.

I've never spoken of him and, although I thought I was sparing your feelings, perhaps I was really sparing my own, and for that I apologise. He gave me the necklace when we parted. It belonged to his mother. I know he would never have parted with it had he not loved me so deeply. I only realise that now. You are like him in so many ways. I know he will love you as much as I do.

I always intended to give you this money regardless of the circumstances. I saved it to help you with whatever you need. Whether that be an education, travel or shoes (I know how much you like shoes).

Happy Birthday, Layla! I'm sorry I could not make it a more special occasion but my heart is with you.

I love you Layla (Eire)
Always
Mummy xoxoxo.

She held her mother's hand and she drifted back to sleep. Now and then, Layla would feel her mother's childlike fingers tighten when she winced in pain; but never a murmur. Layla could feel the pain just as deeply, but she took comfort in knowing her mother would never have intended it so. Her thoughts flitted from her father, to her mother and back to her father. She had no idea who or where he was but never felt the need to know as her mother had always given her enough. At that moment she felt nothing but sympathy for Marie. She could read between the lines: being parted from him had hurt her dreadfully, and she was a constant reminder of him. Layla had no cause to be angry with her; she had suffered enough pain.

Kate stood behind Layla; she appeared from nowhere and Layla started as she rubbed her back. She twisted Layla's blonde hair through her fingers. It was the first time she had shown any sort of affection toward her. Kate seemed deep in thought. In fact, she was admiring the similarities between mother and daughter. Layla had Marie's blonde locks and green eyes, although her flawless milky skin and beautiful features surely came from her father. Marie and Kate had visible similarities too; Kate the darker while Marie the fairer. Layla and Marie with an inner beauty shining through.

Now, though, Marie lay unrecognisable. Kate knew it would not be much longer. She sensed it with every twirl of Layla's hair. She could feel Layla's anxiety but she had no capacity for guilt. Kate did, at that moment, feel some sort of sorrow for her sister, but those feelings passed just as quickly. Kate and John had never been blessed with children. As she watched Layla's hair fall through her fingers, she imagined how her own child would have been very similar to her niece. Losing John had been a living death for her, a living death she had never attempted to escape and most certainly not until she had achieved her objective. Layla's existence gave her reason for being and Marie lying on her deathbed was confirmation enough that Layla's gift was from her father.

'Layla,' Kate whispered, 'the nurse comes this afternoon. Perhaps we could go out to Loch Lomond and get some fresh air.'

Marie opened her eyes, having heard her sister speak. She gestured an insistent nod. Layla had barely left her side for months; she wanted her to go with Kate. Layla brushed her mother's brow with her index finger and agreed to her silent request. Marie stared into her eyes. Layla sensed she was trying to apologise to her but she would not accept an apology. She put her arms delicately around her, being careful not to cause her any pain, and soothed her. A tear fell from Marie's eye onto her cheek. Layla knelt beside her and brushed the tear away.

'If all the mums in the world were lined up I'd still have picked you. You never have to apologise to me,' Layla whispered softly into her mother's ear.

Kate noted Layla's sincerity. This was a great stabilising force when approaching adulthood. Even in Layla's hour of need, Kate's callous thoughts were for her own benefit. She had never chosen to exercise her free will because revenge was too sweet for her. Marie was an obstacle standing in the way. She swore there would never be any distractions until she had settled all scores.

'I love you,' Marie murmured to Layla.

Layla stroked her mother's brow and ran her finger down the bridge of her nose.

'I love you more,' she whispered.

She stroked her mother's face as Marie had stroked hers when she was a child and Marie tried to shake her head in protest; Layla knew she was trying to tell her that *she* was the mother and not the child. Layla smiled, a warm loving smile, as she thought how, even mute, her mother insisted on having the last word.

Marie had her own thoughts. If only Layla knew Marie's deep regret of not seeing her daughter grow older. She wanted to save Layla from the anguish and the fear of dying and of being left alone. She had always been hopeful but that had disappeared; her rapid deterioration had taken her as much by surprise as it had Layla. Marie thought of Connor and hoped Layla would find him to spare her the grief. Connor had given her a precious gift, a tiny flame that would remain lit forever in her soul, Layla!

Kate pulled the Mercedes round to the front of the house and waited for Layla. As Layla got in she hit the accelerator and headed for Loch Lomond. Layla always thought her aunt a reckless driver so she belted up; she didn't particularly like travelling with her. The wheels screeched as the car flew around corners, and through red lights, overtaking cars as if racing in a grand prix. Kate was fearless!

Kate parked the car at Luss, a small village on the edge of the loch. Layla sighed when Kate took the key out of the ignition. She was twiddling her pendant in her fingers to ease her nerves. Her attention drawn, Kate stared at it stonily.

Lofty hills surrounded them as they ambled along the lazy, narrow lanes that wove their way around the loch. They reached the shore front and walked along the T-shaped jetty that jutted out deep into the loch. When they reached the end Layla stood transfixed by the magnificent view. Layla looked into the horizon where rolling hills bordered the wide loch. The water separated them from the patchwork quilt of greenery. The grey water, visible through the gaps in the jetty, splashed below their feet. The water blackened where the depth increased. A speed boat flew past and white waves spread across the loch as water sprayed skyward. Layla was mesmerised. It had been a long time since she had seen so much beauty; there was something wonderful about the freedom of greenery, perhaps the tranquillity.

A wintry, misty haze hung over the loch. The perfume of the purple heather prickled her senses. She sneezed as the perfume blended with the strong fragrances of grass, bark and salt. The scents were unbelievably strong. Aunt Kate pointed to one of the hills, and told her of the ancient legends of Rob Roy and the Highlanders who had once roamed those very fields. Centuries of legacy, tradition and folklore unfolded in the hills before her. With her perfect vision, Layla studied every bush, tree, shrub and rock in fine detail. Despite the mist, she saw the distinctive outline of a man in the distance, a man larger than life. He looked familiar but, as she blinked, he disappeared. She assumed that the distance must have thrown up a kind of mirage; she was mystified – everything had seemed so clear. She tried to retrace the shape again but suddenly she felt a tap on her shoulder. She started; it was her aunt.

'Sorry, I was in another world,' Layla said.

'I noticed,' Aunt Kate grinned. 'They say they still roam there!'

Layla could feel her body tense.

'Who?'

'The Highlanders,' Kate answered.

They walked back along the jetty, but Layla kept looking back. The figure did not reappear, and she wondered if her mind had been playing tricks on her. She decided to put it out of her mind and occupied herself by admiring the floral baskets hanging outside the small cottages strewn throughout the village. To her right was a hotel that looked more like a large log cabin on stilts, with huge windows so people could look out at the charming view. Through the panes of glass she could make out a few figures and Layla hoped they weren't a figment of her imagination too.

Kate a few paces in front, led Layla along a dusty path that ran adjacent to the shore. By the time they reached a small incline she had caught up with her aunt. They were walking past an old church, its age given away by the Viking grave which lay in the graveyard; the mound mimicked the underside of a Viking boat. They stood gazing at it in silence, and then walked along a winding, natural path of coloured leaves to the back of the church. Leaves fell from the overhanging trees and into a stream that ran into the loch. As they stood on a small footbridge neither of them was aware that the other was counting each leaf as it dropped and was carried away by the stream.

The clouds merged in the sky and then darkened to a murky grey. Seconds passed and the rain poured. Layla sprinted to the car but her jaw dropped as her aunt darted in front of her. Water dripped from their hair, clinging to their faces, and their saturated clothes hugged their bodies, revealing their animal-like splendour. They climbed into the car and glanced at one another without uttering a word. More seconds passed as they stared out the window and watched the rain splash off the bonnet of the Mercedes.

'Are you hungry?' Aunt Kate asked.

Layla looked at the small village shop.

'I could murder a steak,' she answered.

Her aunt revelled in the changes that were taking place in her niece but she kept her thoughts to herself.

'You spent far too long in South Africa. Honestly, they must have cholesterol levels through the roof!'

Aunt Kate sniggered as she waited for Layla's reaction. Layla didn't flinch.

Kate put her foot to the floor, speeding once again along the winding roads; splashing through large puddles in the road. Layla fastened her seatbelt and braced herself. Kate smiled.

As the rain continued to fall the puddles quickly stretched across the breadth of the road. Layla watched as each drop hit the windscreen and wondered how there could be a forecast for even more rain. She didn't mind the cold, but the constant pitter-patter drove her insane. They were passing a large, enclosed field when Layla noticed a sign for the next Highland Games. She remembered Duncan and Ewan inviting her to join them at various events many times before. They attended traditional gatherings obsessively; they were true Scotsmen with a passion for their home country that seemed unquenchable.

The return route seemed longer. Layla was feeling frustrated; she wanted to get back to her mother. Every tick of Layla's watch sounded louder and louder and louder in her ears; she felt annoyed when Kate stopped at a butcher's on the way home. 'Freshest in Town' it stated above the shop. When finally she returned to the car Layla could have sworn that the meat she carried had been caught and slaughtered especially for her aunt. The smell was fresh and strangely tantalising.

By the time they reached home and her aunt was circling the surrounding streets trying to find a parking place, Layla's patience had worn thin. As Kate finally slowed down, Layla sprang from the car and in a split second had dashed out of sight and into the house.

Kate watched her dispassionately, congratulating herself on how shrewd she'd been. She opened the glove compartment and looked at the black, leather-bound diary; she patted her fingers on it, pleased with the content. It gave her the extra information she needed to finalise her plans. Marie asked her to keep the diary for Layla, when she was older but she had no intention of giving it to her.

When she entered the house, Layla stood before her for a moment blank-faced and then turned and went back into Marie's room. Kate followed. She already knew what lay inside.

Layla almost willed herself to cry and yet she could not. Instead she stared at her mother's body, youthful once more, sleeping beauty with all the pain erased from her face.

2

Regan

The plane landed in Glasgow International and Regan sighed. Flying was bottom of his list as a chosen mode of transport. He liked his feet placed firmly on the ground. He wondered how in the world he'd made it across the Atlantic in the first place. If he'd had more time – if he'd not needed to enrol and pay a fee deposit at college – he would have chosen to travel by rail, bus or even on foot. Timing wasn't the only reason; his venturing from city to city had eventually caused his feet to fail him. He had blisters on top of blisters and so had decided to hang his walking boots up for a while.

Regan's intention was always to return to the US to complete his studies but by going to Glasgow he avoided another gruelling flight, with the added bonus of avoiding another gruelling fight with his parents. Both these reasons had made his choice of Glasgow University easier. There was a certain irony to it all, since impulsiveness was not part of his nature. Perhaps the gap year had changed something in him; then again, it could have been the two impetuous Irishmen he'd befriended. He met his two new friends while working in Bruges. Regan usually resisted peer pressure, but his two Irish friends most certainly had the gift of the gab. They were very persuasive and convinced him to enrol at Glasgow

University by charming him into believing it would be a great adventure.

Although there had been many changes in Regan since he'd begun his explorations, he hadn't lost complete leave of his senses. He had worked while travelling so the balance of his savings account was now impressive. His healthy bank balance had even enabled him to buy a car. His father, too, transferred money into his account regularly, in quite generous amounts. At least he was generous with his finances, if nothing else, Regan thought.

Regan pulled his new red Fiesta up to the kerb on Byers Road. He was calculating how much more expensive the cars were in the UK compared with the States. He knew Ford, so he stuck with the all-American brand, though he'd expected a car with a little more space for the price. All the same, it raced from A to B so he put his penny-pinching on the backburner.

Franky and Kite liked speed and as they walked over to the car from outside the entrance to the Metro station they nodded their approval. They did look a little disgruntled but their impatience had been something he'd learned to accept.

'Bout ye, Yank?' Franky said as he opened the door of the passenger side.

Regan was getting used to some of the slang they threw in with their otherwise well-spoken English.

'Thought you'd gone to America to get your car,' Kite said and laughed.

'My flight was delayed,' Regan said.

'Ah, so you did go to America, land of Ford. You could have brought something a little bigger back with you. I thought all you Yanks like big, flashy motors,' Kite laughed.

'You two are – what is it you say again – a gag,' Regan said.

They laughed at Regan's attempts to act as they did.

Regan laughed too. He laughed with them and at them.

'You guys don't look too good,' he said, and pointed at Franky, who looked even paler than usual.

'Freshers' week,' Kite explained. 'Franky's hopeless when it comes to Bloody Marys,' he sniggered.

Regan laughed and nodded to Kite.

'You look like you're about to ...' Regan hadn't finished the sentence when Franky threw up, splattering Kite's shoes.

Regan pursed his lips to contain his laughter.

'Ugh ... Franky, what the ...!' Kite said.

He retched, turned away, and then retched again.

Franky was trying to clean himself up. Kite threw his shoes off and jumped into the passenger seat of Regan's car.

'You can't get in now!' Regan insisted. 'I just bought this car.'

'No, I'm grand now, honest! I'm just thirsty,' Franky said.

Regan couldn't see much change in the colour of his face, so he wasn't so sure Franky was being honest. Before he had time to object, Franky threw his rucksack into the back of the car and got in.

Regan looked puzzled as he looked at the rucksack. He could never understand how they could possibly travel so light. He thought about it for a moment and then remembered how infrequently they changed their clothes, which forced him to question how on earth they didn't smell like old boots. He had not realised he was shaking his head until he saw his two friends glaring at him. As he slowed the movement to an eventual stop, he realised they were anything but normal.

Kite turned his attention to the radio. He fiddled and turned up the volume. Kite drummed on the dashboard to the beat of the music and whooped.

'Welcome to the jungle, boys,' he bellowed. 'It's time for this kite to fly. Kite by name; Kite by nature!'

'Do you have another name?' Regan shouted. Kite blocked his ears.

'All right, there's no need to shout,' he said. Regan couldn't hear anything except the loud beat battering his ears. He reached over and turned down the volume. Kite didn't seem to object.

Franky spoke.

'Aye, you Yanks don't think anything of being called Dick or Candy; but where we come from they are names for other things. Kite, however, is a very acceptable name.'

Regan laughed, knowing full well what 'dick' was but 'candy' baffled him.

'You say sweets,' he said innocently.

Franky and Kite guffawed.

Regan frowned, embarrassed and confused. He was a little naive and it frustrated him. They found it highly amusing. He hoped they didn't know how inexperienced he really was. He assumed if they had any idea they would have made his life not worth living; mocking him at given opportunity.

'Live and learn, Yank,' Franky said. 'Candy involves more sweat than sweets!'

'Oh!'

Franky and Kite rolled laughing again.

'Frank by name; jerk by nature!'

'That's pretty quick by your standards, Yankee. A bit like Tommy here,' Franky laughed.

'You're an ass, Franky,' Kite said scornfully.

'You love me really, Kiteman,' Franky laughed.

'No one calls me Tommy. I'm Kite as in "as high as". I like to climb, Yank, and soar!' Kite smiled.

'You're crazy,' Regan laughed.

'I like to think of myself as unique. Could be worse though, I could be Franky; he's more of a glider,' Kite said.

He glimpsed behind him at Franky.

'Are you two into extreme sports?' Regan asked, becoming animated.

'Aye, something like that,' Kite said.

He rolled his eyes. Franky's frame quivered as he struggled to stop laughing.

Franky and Kite were the polar opposites of Regan; chalk to his cheese.

'Hey, Regan,' Kite spurted, 'Franky and I were talking the other day. We wanted to ask you to come back to Glenarm with us for a long weekend. We're from a wee village in the back of beyond and we thought you might like to see why we're so "out of control" when we're let out.'

Regan parked the car outside the student halls and turned to Kite. Kite exchanged a surreptitious look with Franky, and Franky laughed quietly.

'That's very generous of you,' he said.

After he said the words he thought about his brother and how these two strangers reminded him of Jimmy, and how much he missed him. He had always been so generous with Regan. Seven years had passed since James had been lost at sea. The years had passed in the blink of an eye, but still he did not lose hope. He would dream it was a mistake; one part of him wanted nothing more than to cross the Irish Sea to feel closer to his brother, but another did not want to reignite the grief. Over the years he had come up with a whole raft of scenarios: his parents had kept James from returning, or he was suffering from amnesia. But, in truth, they were just excuses for Regan to bypass the truth.

Kite and Franky were sitting in silence, observing Regan's trancelike state. As soon as he'd snapped out of it, they helped him with his luggage but oddly didn't hang around. Franky was looking paler than ever.

Regan unlocked the door of his dormitory, entered the room and studied every detail of the small box room. His room at home was enormous in comparison, but he'd never felt happy there. Now he felt a wave of contentment wash over him. He hadn't felt that way for a long time. Images of his home life crept into his mind. His mother drinking herself into an oblivion (she'd fallen apart after Jimmy went missing). His father spending all his time at the office or entertaining other women. Regan felt like he had escaped.

Franky and Kite never seemed to ask about his family or his life in America. They only ever seemed interested in him and the future. It made for a pleasant change but he guessed that, if they saw his world, or rather, the one he had come from, they might not have seen him in the same light, or invited him into theirs. He sighed. He felt a little guilty having never mentioned his family. In fact, he'd made a point of convincing them he was alone in the world – that, after all, was how he felt.

A couple of hours later Kite walked in. He was averse to knocking and Regan had adapted to this violation of his privacy.

'Right, Yank … are you up for your initiation now? Franky's feeling better … so get your kit on,' he said, slapping Regan's back with enthusiasm.

'Ow!'

'Ooh … sorry, brother … I don't know my own strength,' Kite said.

'I thought you were going for something to eat?' Regan asked.

'No. I'm fine. It was Franky who needed nourishment … Nothing new there!'

Regan wondered about Kite's use of vocabulary at times and remembered how odd he could be.

'Well … are you coming?' Kite asked impatiently.

'No thanks. I need to unpack and sleep. I feel like I haven't slept for a month.'

Regan liked his alone time. He found Kite and Franky intense at times; Franky particularly.

'Are you wise? This is freshers' week … You're *supposed* to get wrecked and find someone to give you some candy,' Kite said.

Kite knew his answer before he said it.

'I'm allergic to alcohol,' Regan said. 'We've had this conversation quite a few times ...' Regan lied convincingly. It was his mother's drinking habits that was the real cause of his teetotalism.

'Obviously you're allergic to girls too,' Kite joked. 'You don't seem particularly interested in the opposite, dare I say it, sex. Umm ... you don't fancy me, do you?' Kite chuckled.

Regan laughed hysterically.

'Trust me,' he said, 'if I was looking for a man, you would not be him. But thanks for the kind offer.'

'Offer?'

Kite grabbed the door handle, making a quick exit. Regan gave a camp wave and blew him a kiss; Kite ignored him and pulled the door behind him. He scowled, making his way down the corridor. Regan laughed. He knew that would get Kite offside.

3

Protective Leon

Leon moulded his tall, ebony frame against the church steeple that stretched high into the night sky. He remained inconspicuous to all who walked the pavements below as his shadow merged into the dark and starless sky.

He watched Layla as she weaved in and out, going against the tide of the human traffic. They were heading to the pubs and clubs while she was rushing to get home. Leon could have timed her. She walked with such precision and never strayed from her route. He'd counted ten minutes as she turned from Great Western Road into Byers Road.

A creature of habit, he thought.

She walked the same route to and from school daily and he wondered how she would feel about the change she would have to make to her route when she attended Glasgow University. She would have to walk in the opposite direction at different intervals for different lectures.

Leon knew Layla as intimately as any stranger could. He had spent the entirety of her seventeen years hiding in her shadows and ensuring her safety. He wanted nothing more than to reveal himself to her but he could only observe; those were his instructions. He had promised her father all those years before that he would protect Layla and her mother. Connor could not risk leaving Amara, fearing she would search for him and discover Layla's existence.

Leon had the ability to walk the streets day or night, but he could not allow Layla to recognise him. Even for her to suspect his presence would have blown his cover. By remaining invisible he could catch sight of any who walked her path. He had seen one or two of his kind in her presence over the years, but since they had posed no threat to her he'd never intervened. Since she'd been living in Scotland the sightings had been few and far between because there was more danger for his kind in Scotland. By making themselves visible they would only have brought unnecessary strife to all who'd dared to cross the Scottish border and remained hidden among the so-called humanity.

'The thirst': his one basic need. Consuming fresh blood was the price of his immortality. The metallic salty liquid was his sole means of survival, since without it he became weak and eventually trapped in an endless paralysis. Leon embraced his vampirism. He believed it had its merits because he felt little pain. If he received any wounds they healed almost immediately. He was a very powerful vampire given he'd only been around for a hundred years … Leon licked his lips, remembering he hadn't fed for a while.

A sudden gust of wind. The weathervane above him spun wildly and he covered his ears. He would watch just a while longer.

When he spotted two forms shadowing Layla he was glad he hadn't left prematurely. He watched closely, trying to see what their eyes would tell him. He wasn't sure what kind of lifestyle these had chosen, though he was certain they were one of his kind. Had they integrated themselves as everyday Glaswegians? But when he caught a glimpse of their dark eyes, he knew immediately: they consumed just as he did and it caused him concern.

He snarled as he wondered how creatures with such vast

minds could be so foolish to walk uninhibited among humans. His face changed to a frown when he saw how cleverly they kept their distance from Layla. An electric shock shot through him as he registered the imminent danger she was in. Without hesitation, he leapt in one fluid movement from the steeple to the opposite rooftop. As he landed, he knocked a tile from the roof; his hunger had made him clumsy. After three further leaps, he was down on the street below, but another roof tile followed him, clattering noisily onto the pavement below.

Ignoring the startled cries of the passers-by Leon took to his heels and homed his hearing in on Layla's breathing. He sprinted; he didn't like her out of sight.

He reached the outskirts of the park in front of Layla's home and hid against a wall of an adjacent house. He waited for her, as impatient as ever, staring into the park in front of him. It was a large green square bordered by tall trees and a wrought-iron fence.

Had he been breathing he would have sighed when he saw her approaching. He had to keep reminding himself not to intervene; in his current state he wasn't strong enough to overpower the two vampires.

Thankfully the surrounding streets and the park were busy that evening. Young couples, families and elderly folk were meandering along the footpaths while others sat on benches or lay dotted about the grass. Humans in Glasgow were never deterred by the weather; if they had been they would rarely have ventured outdoors. The scent of humans would be distracting for the vampires and they would not pick up on his.

Leon noted that the two vampires weren't obviously threatening toward Layla. They seemed to be just observing her from afar. Leon watched, almost with amusement, as he noticed their eyes focusing on the other humans as they came too close. Some people sensed the interest and turned to look at them, oblivious to the danger they were putting themselves in. Though excited, the vampires held back, and Leon thought their caution strange. They did not seem naturally restrained; their eyes had told him that.

As soon as Layla entered her home and closed the door behind her, the vampires left with gusto. They reached the end of the street and were quickly out of sight, sprinting and jumping through the air as Leon followed them. As he passed Layla's house, he slowed down a little, looking for a glimpse of Marie.

Leon looked around the square as he left, noting how affluent the surrounding houses seemed. He thought back to the basic houses and apartments Layla and her mother usually lived in and his mind raced, wondering how they could suddenly have afforded such a beautiful home.

Spotting the vampires ahead, Leon kept his distance as he sprinted along rooftops and soared through trees. As he reached Great Western Road he watched the two vampires scale the fence of the cricket grounds. In the background he could see the city hospital, a place he was so familiar with. He stopped for a moment and then walked across the green to the perimeter fence. He knew where they were going.

The vampires had unnerved him and he knew that soon he would have to find a way to be nearer to Layla. The danger felt too close to stay hiding in the shadows. But what would he do? He would think of something once he, too, had quenched his thirst. He jumped the fence and dashed round to the rear entrance of the hospital with thoughts whirling in his mind.

4

Friends

Layla's senses, perceptions and intuitions sharpened with the intensity of her emotions. Her aunt could feel her pain, but she had no regrets. It simply reminded her of her own complex anguish when she had lost John. She had bided her time, been patient and cautious; she needed Layla alone! Since she had achieved that objective, she needed to earn her trust and support and help her change. As she looked at her pale, milky exterior she felt relief as her eyes began to vary between dark olives and emeralds; it was infrequent, but it still occurred. There was another sign, not obvious to the untrained eye, but which Kate recognised as marking the completion of another phase. The symptoms remained too subtle for Layla to spot but they would inevitably lead to a further stage … denial.

Layla awoke, wanting nothing more than to fall back into her slumber; the dream comforted her and she yearned for it after the loss of her mother. She missed her so much that it physically pained her, but she vowed to remain strong; she had never broken a promise to her. At times she felt numb; at others irrational, unmotivated and overwhelmed. Her mind flitted regularly from one thought to another. She tried her best to focus her attention on reality.

Layla heard the two hormone-imbalanced adolescents

making a racket downstairs. It was a gentle reminder for her to hurry along. She washed, dressed and hoped going out would slow the spiralling motion in her head. She flew downstairs, pulling on the banister to slow any sudden movements; she had an abundance of energy to burn, and she never seemed to tire. She assumed moping around the house and not burning off any energy had affected her sleep.

'Morning,' Ewan said.

She always admired his warm Scottish brogue and husky tones. He jumped up from the sofa and hugged her, brushing her cheek lightly with his soft lips.

'Ooh cold,' he said.

His eyes watered as he looked at her and he caught her captivating scent in his nose.

'Morning,' she sang.

She touched her throat; she was hoarse. Her voice must have broken into a more womanly one; it sounded strange hearing her own voice so clearly. The boys were oblivious to it, too busy admiring her. Feeling slightly uncomfortable as their eyes lingered, she went through to the kitchen to make coffee.

'Would either of you like a coffee?' she called.

'Yeah great!'

She had an uncontrollable need for fluids and she drank her coffee strong; she liked the strong aroma and the bitter taste. She wondered if it, too, could have affected her sleep pattern. She had always been a bit of an insomniac, but never so severely. She ignored the ringing in her ears and went back into the living room with the boys' coffees. Her appetite had diminished but she assumed it was the amount of fluids she drank. She had an incessant need for caffeine and the caffeine coursing her veins often gave her the jitters. Her craving for alcohol didn't help either. She had rarely drank before but now she found herself taking swigs of brandy from her aunt's decanter. Apparently brandy settled her stomach, which otherwise felt permanently in knots, and it did seem to help. She often attempted to use willpower to limit her consumption but she could not reduce the cravings and that only added to her ambivalent instability.

Duncan spoke; his deep voice grounded her. He rolled his *r*s in the same way Ewan did. She never tired of the deep, gruff manner in which they spoke.

'Don't dawdle, Layla; we'd like to leave on time for a change,' he said. 'Try not to get lost in the wardrobe or anything like that.'

Layla could hear him snorting, amused by his own sense of humour.

'You're hilarious, Dunc,' she said. 'As you can see, I'm already dressed and, besides, Megan's not even here yet. I've just my pearly-whites to brush and I'm set.'

Ewan watched them as their usual verbal tennis match ensued; nothing unusual about that. Duncan had taken the first serve as he normally did.

'Ugh ... would you ever calm down? ... You know I'm right. You'll get upstairs and realise you have your hair to brush. Then decide to paint your nails and tie your laces. Oh and then pack your handbag, put on your coat and do it all over again. Then as we're about to leave, you're sure to have forgotten something. Do I need to go on? Oh, and one more thing: STOP CALLING ME DUNC!'

'Oh flowers of Scotland!' Ewan intervened. 'You two act more like mortal enemies than friends. She only calls you Dunc to wind you up.'

He looked at Duncan wondering how anyone could be so childish. He and Layla were both laughing hysterically.

'Flowers of Scotland?' Duncan roared. 'Bloody hell ... what's that all about?'

'Thistles,' Ewan said, 'and less of the foul language in the presence of a lady!'

'She's no lady!' Duncan winked at Layla.

'You're relentless,' Ewan said.

'Now who's getting wound up, Ewy?' Duncan chuckled.

'Ugh.'

Ewan had to rise above Duncan's remarks; it was pointless … he never gave up.

'Thanks for trying, Ewan,' Layla said.

She turned to Duncan.

'There was I thinking chivalry was dead, although Dunc may well be trying to kill it!'

Layla smirked and hurtled upstairs to escape Duncan's wrath.

'NOT DUNC!'

Baffled, Duncan stared at the empty stairs and wiped his eyes. He was sure they must have been playing tricks on him. Ewan was so busy splitting his sides laughing, he didn't even notice Layla go upstairs.

The two boys, best friends, were more like brothers growing together and learning the riches of their heritage. Duncan's family were the poorer relations in comparison to Ewan's, who owned an estate in the Highlands. Duncan's uncle, Frazer, managed the estate and the boys spent every other weekend with him. They both called him 'Uncle', although Ewan was a MacGregor, as in Rob Roy, and he regularly reminded Duncan of the fact – he being a McDonald. But they *were* related, both being full-bred Scotsmen and as they grew older *that* became more important to them. They were so different, in looks and personality, but they had the same strong Scottish values and beliefs. They loved and respected everything about Scotland and its people. Although they attended school in the Lowlands and spent most of their time in and around Glasgow, they never accepted being referred to as 'lowlanders'. Their roots remained firmly in the Highlands.

Layla brushed her hair then tied it back. She applied a touch of foundation after she looked in the mirror and noticed her pale reflection. She glossed her lips and darkened her lashes, simply to finish the job. Suddenly she saw the shining of her eyes. The sun must be strong, she thought. It was catching the green in her eyes. Then her vision sharpened. It startled her. The mirror was moving closer. She blinked and stumbled backward, landing on her bed. She lay back blinking numerous times; she felt dizzy and disoriented. Probably an ear infection, she thought; she was sure that affected balance. She rolled two pieces of cotton wool in her hand and pushed the balls into her ears. She giggled to herself, realising it would not only keep out the cold but muffle Duncan's jibes too.

Megan arrived on time; they all gave each other a squeeze.

'Layla, not so hard,' Megan said.

'Sorry! I didn't realise I was hugging you so tightly,' Layla said.

They left to catch the Underground to the city's centre. The wind nipped at their heels as they walked; they welcomed the shelter as they went down the escalator chatting. The train arrived just as they reached the platform; they got on and the doors closed.

The train was full so Layla was standing holding the silver rail above her head. The whooshing sound of the automatic doors hypnotised her as she daydreamed about Glasgow and her friends. She used the security of her relationships with her friends. They had no idea how much they helped her to cope with her grief. They had been so welcoming to her from day one when she enrolled at Glasgow Academy. They folded her into the group, even though she was a foreigner. But then she wasn't English, although her accent threw them at first. She soon learned to pick up a slightly more Glaswegian accent. They had almost encircled her and taken her under their protection. Her final thought before Megan pinched her lightly as the doors whooshed and she followed them off the train.

They walked along Sauchiehall Street, the main pedestrian thoroughfare of the city. The boys decided shopping with indecisive girls would probably be best avoided.

'We'll meet you for lunch. Unless, of course, you need some help in the changing rooms?' Duncan said. He winked at them.

'No thanks,' Megan replied curtly.

Duncan was tactless but witty, and Megan regularly fell into his camouflaged traps.

'We might head to some of the more interesting shops, like Virgin,' he said.

And he and Ewan walked off laughing.

'Layla,' Megan said, and then cupped her hand around her mouth and whispered, 'Is it even called Virgin any more?'

'No, Megan … you bite every time!'

They laughed as they walked along the pavement nattering. The walkways were busy; people bustled past one another in crisscross style. Layla, being the more observant, noticed the vagrants, like menacing sprites, as they shouted erratic profanities or greetings, whichever took their fancy, and swigged on bottles of cheap booze and spirits. Layla imagined how easy it would be to get lost in a city like Glasgow. But she soon became distracted by Megan's incessant talking about Ewan. Layla returned her attention to her, but wished she had stayed in her trance; she knew where the conversation was going. Layla had her suspicions, she thought perhaps Megan was checking for any competition.

'Ewan is rugged and good looking and *soooo* charming!'

Layla nodded.

She waited for Megan to add how attractive girls found him. Then, right on time, as though Megan was reading an autocue, she mentioned how girls found him so attractive.

'Duncan's such a ladies' man. I find him so arrogant. He just can't seem to help himself, can he? The dirty dog!'

And Megan went on and on and on.

Layla remained silent. She didn't find Duncan arrogant; he made her laugh and he would have been devastated if he thought he'd really offended either of them. Megan, in contrast to Layla, saw him more as man's best friend as opposed to woman's.

Suddenly a look of terror covered Megan's face. At first Layla thought she was annoyed with her for not answering her question. It was only when she heard the horrific screams ripping through her ears and forced herself to turn around that she witnessed what had shocked Megan.

A sprite lay writhing on the pavement with the neck of an empty spirits bottle protruding from *his* throat. He'd been transformed into a lowly man, as his dangerous blood spilled over the pavement. It was a puddle of deep claret. Megan ran to the victim. She knelt beside him. Her knees became soaked in the pool of blood. The red liquid kept spurting from him and splattered Megan's light-blue coat as she tried to stop the flow with her hands.

'RING AN AMBULANCE! SOMEONE RING AN AMBULANCE!'

She pulled the scarf from her neck and wrapped it around his. She kept applying pressure to the wound as Layla stood staring, frozen. She could not process what was happening. It felt like she was no longer in her body or she was watching from another level. She could not breathe; her heart palpitated, her pulse raced; she could hear it beating in her ears along with his. His heartbeat was faint and fading. She could feel her body going into a cold sweat.

'Oh no please! Not another panic attack … not now!' Layla heard herself saying out loud, but thankfully no one was paying much attention. They were too preoccupied with the unfolding horror. She took deep breaths.

Megan was shouting again asking for someone to help her, or to do something. She ripped her coat from her back and placed it over the victim. She lay over his body trying to raise his body temperature while he shivered uncontrollably. Megan knew she should not remove the broken bottle or he would bleed out more rapidly. The alcohol coursing his veins made his blood more fluid; Layla had already caught the scent of both as they scratched at her throat.

'Layla, give me your coat … Layla, come on, focus!'

Layla could see the blood draining from his face. She ran and stopped just close enough to throw her coat to Megan. Then ignoring the ringing in her ears, and the burning in her throat, she held her breath and dashed forward to help Megan. The man's life was spilling from him as another woman sat alongside her. She took his hand in hers. In silent unison all three knew they were helpless to save him. Finally, a drone in the distance; Layla picked it up. She could hear it getting closer, faster.

'The ambulance is coming,' she said.

Megan looked at her, confused. She could hear nothing. She pressed on his chest, trying to administer CPR, and Layla aided his breathing. Her insides churned as she resisted the unthinkable. Megan heard the ambulance as it drew closer. It screeched to a halt and the paramedics ran to aid the victim. They stood back. Tears ran down Megan's face and landed on her blood-soaked clothes and as she wiped her tears, her hand covered her face in blood. The crowd watched as his body finally convulsed. Layla had known his fate when she noticed the glass protruding from his jugular. A victim of circumstance, he would soon be forgotten, and his drunken behaviour seen as the justification for his death.

The paramedics covered his body when the police arrived. Why were they never about when they were needed? Layla felt angry. The white cloth clung to his lifeless body and coloured pink almost instantly, then turned crimson. She and Megan were taken to the ambulance. Megan didn't seem to be running on adrenalin at that point. Instead she was in shock. Layla wanted to disappear; she found the ferocity gripping, and it frightened her. The observers dispersed; no one witnessed the homicide; that would have been far too inconvenient. The police offered her a lift and after giving a short statement and Megan a hug, she got into the back of the police car and Megan was taken to hospital by ambulance.

When the police car pulled up outside her aunt's house the policemen took her contact number in case there were any further enquiries. She sprang from the vehicle and pushed the door shut behind her. She choked. She gulped a mouthful of air. She'd been holding her breath for what felt like an age. She watched the police car turn from her sight and wondered if anyone would be brought to justice without her statement. The image flashed in front of her; she shuddered as she recalled his silent departure. To the other witnesses he had seemed to be just another bystander, a duplicate of the victim, but she had seen behind the grimy stains disguising the young, pallid face. At first it had been a blur but then her vision had focused and magnified each feature of his malevolent face. He had no soul. The distinct and yet unfamiliar form, beyond a shadow of doubt, was a foe. She could never reveal such an implausible tale to the police. She had probed Megan who did not mention seeing anyone.

Layla's panic attacks were becoming more severe; they seemed to include hallucinations that were taking on an ever stronger degree of reality. Her mind went into overload as she remembered the hush, his speed and swift agility. It seemed absurd. Now she wanted to scream – had this trauma tipped her over the edge? Had she stared so intensely into the abyss that it in turn had stared back at her? Layla hoped forensic evidence would give the police a link to the perpetrator of the violence. It would make things so much more plausible and stop the velocity of the spinning in her head. Was it shock, distress or hormones? Or was she losing her mind? She struggled to find an answer.

Aunt Kate was clattering crockery in the kitchen, her usual little façade of busy domesticity. There always seemed to be a mountain of dishes. Layla used Kate's apparent pre-occupation to sneak upstairs. She wanted to wash and change and keep her blood-spattered face from her aunt. Layla would mention the incident but she needed time to think. Nothing made sense to her and spouting a pile of nonsense could have caused her aunt to overreact.

Layla climbed into bed, hiding below the covers. She did not sleep but the darkness, warmth and familiar smell of her covers gave her security. It helped drive out the incessant shivering of her body. She tried to distract herself, her mother, the dream, the boys, but the chasm inside her head kept widening, obscuring any chance of clarity. She heard her aunt creeping along the hallway so she imitated sleep when she peeked into her room. The door closed. Layla's actions were her way of communicating and Kate knew she needed space.

Layla scraped her way out from under her covers as dawn broke. Kate knew it was too soon to probe her; she hoped Layla had the strength to overturn the uncertainty.

More rattling.

Layla watched Kate from a distance. She considered the similarities between Kate and her mother, who were the image of one another, only in different hues. Kate allowed her a lot more freedom than her mother would have and, although it gave her the opportunity to discover herself, sometimes she wished she was a little more rigid. Aunt Kate seemed to view her in a clear light yet somehow she seemed to lurk in the shadows.

'Morning!'

Kate turned to acknowledge Layla. Her voice was full and rich as if she were trying to alleviate the stark shade in Layla's eyes.

'Morning!' Layla was a little more subdued.

'Did you go into the city yesterday?' she asked as she stared into Layla's eyes.

'Yeah,' she said.

Layla broke her aunt's gaze and walked into the living room. She sat on a chair beside the window. Her ears pricked up with the sound of muffled crying. She shuffled, uncomfortable, and shook her head lightly. Then she heard another voice, a comforting voice together with the tiny voice that was griping again. Layla noticed the mum on the opposite side of the road, trying to strap her baby into a car seat. The little round face was red in protest, her tiny frame tensed. She was refusing to be restrained. Her mother soothed her but her tone became impatient. Layla giggled at the wilfulness of the child. The scene made her think of Marie's similar tactics with her. The frustrated mum finally snapped at the tot; she'd lost her patience. Layla could feel her own temperament change but as the baby relaxed, more contented, her annoyance eased. Amazing, she thought, that someone so small could already know she had pushed her mother far enough. Layla remembered knowing Marie's limits. There was a second sharp snap, but it was the buckle of the car seat. The mum kissed the baby's chubby dimpled cheek, tapped her button nose and smiled.

'Good girl,' she said.

A playful, tiny giggle was the reply and it warmed Layla's temperament. She saw the unconditional love in the baby's bright eyes as she beamed with innocence. Layla could smell her scent; the smell of a baby could surely have been bottled and sold for profit. Layla touched her forehead, her nose, and remembered the warmth of her mother's touch. It remained embedded within her. The slam of the car door brought her back from her daydream. She felt soothed, having witnessed something so warm and wonderful. She wanted to hold on to that.

Layla remembered her aunt telling her how dramatically

she had changed when she lost her husband, John. Kate told her that she knew time would ease the physical pain but she would never forget. Layla believed her; she'd seen the anguish in Kate when she spoke of John. Layla kept hold of her memories and intended to for ever.

Layla went back into the kitchen where her aunt was waiting patiently. Kate decided that keeping on Layla's good side would be of far more benefit to her. She had a game plan and it needed to be played properly.

'What's wrong, sweetheart? You look like you've seen a ghost!'

Aunt Kate moved closer as she analysed her.

'I did,' Layla said.

'What? You saw a ghost!'

Aunt Kate rubbed the middle of her brow.

'Aunt Kate, you look like you're the one seeing the ghost,' Layla chuckled.

'I'm just um … I'm not finding any of this very funny,' Aunt Kate said.

She didn't mean to sound so abrupt.

Layla had never seen her aunt take that tone. 'Sorry,' she whispered.

She questioned whether confiding in her aunt would be the right move after all.

'Sorry, sweetheart! I think I overreacted. You caught me unaware,' she said.

Kate sensed Layla's unease and wanted to stop her clamming up. It was important.

'You know how I went into the city centre with Megan yesterday,' Layla said.

'And Duncan and Ewan,' her aunt added. Ooh, she deserved an award for this, she thought, trying to concentrate more intently on the conversation as well as showing that she was.

'Well … um … yes, but we split up,' Layla said.

'Aye, the boys usually do that!'

'Yes that wasn't unusual. When Megan and I were walking along Buchanan Street we saw a man injured. I saw …'

Layla cut her sentence short, unsure if she should include her visions. No, not at that juncture, she concluded.

'Oh, yes I saw the news, something brief about it. What happened to him?'

Layla remained silent.

'But what's a ghost got to do with any of it?' Kate insisted, realising that staring at Layla with pretended disbelief was harder than she thought. 'What happened? I mean things like that never happen in broad daylight and not in one of the busiest streets in Glasgow,' Kate babbled.

'He seemed to get into a fight.'

'OK, that's not so unusual in this city,' Aunt Kate sighed.

'I froze,' she paused. She was finding it hard to speak freely, but she needed to tell someone. 'Um … initially I found it all a bit strange. I helped him as much as I could, but there was something odd. I could smell the alcohol but the smell of the blood…' Layla cleared her throat. '… The salty, metallic scent stung my throat,' Layla said as she shuddered.

'But you helped in an awful situation. We don't all have the constitution for blood,' Aunt Kate said.

'Yes, but there's more.'

Aunt Kate remained silent as she rubbed Layla's arm, trying to help ease her distress.

'I knew it would be pointless,' Layla said as she bit her bottom lip, 'the bottle had been pushed so deep into his main artery and the blood was spouting everywhere. It looked brutal.'

Aunt Kate's jaw fell open.

'In his neck … Are you sure?' Her voice went up a note or two.

'Yes, certain! We … I saw it done! I knew he was beyond help.'

'Back up a minute, why did you change "we saw" to "I saw"?' Aunt Kate said. She softened her tone to put Layla at ease.

'No one else saw who did it but me,' Layla explained simply.

Layla looked into her aunt's eyes, trying to understand what she was thinking.

'How did you get home, Layla?' she asked.

'With the police,' Layla said.

Aunt Kate gasped.

'I said nothing. I couldn't! They would never have believed me. How could only *one* person have seen someone? I think I'm having hallucinations,' she said.

Her aunt listened intently but she did not react.

'Do you think I'm losing my mind? I checked the Internet and hallucinating is not a good sign. I have strange symptoms. I know Mom didn't have any problems like that but that could be why she left my dad, couldn't it?' she said.

Layla was really upset.

Aunt Kate put her arms around her. This was not what Layla expected, but she needed the affection.

'To be honest, everything's a blur. This all feels real, like it all exists, but it's impossible.'

'Layla, trust me, just calm down; you need time. We will come up with an answer. For now it's an erratic time for you and that's to be expected. Think of it being like a woman's period. Every female takes a different amount of time to complete her cycle.'

She was gaining Layla's trust and that was important.

'Is that a roundabout way of telling me I'm growing up?'

'Yes, you're maturing and I'll help you. It wasn't *so* long ago that I too had to go through the same process.'

Layla felt the tension ease from her body as her aunt soothed her. She felt like a small child.

'All my senses are so sharp; it's scary. That's why I said nothing to the police; they would have thought I was lying.'

Aunt Kate gave Layla her full attention.

'I felt every emotion and my mind went out of control. I thought I could hear his thoughts but it may have been voices. I hear a lot of voices and noises. They're crystal clear, in stereo, and sometimes they're far away. It switches off and on.'

Layla felt convinced her aunt thought she was insane because she just listened. She didn't comment on anything. She decided she needed some time alone and excused herself.

Her aunt let her go. She had to take her time. The process was not predictable, more so with Layla. Just keeping an eye on her was all she could do at that point.

The following day Layla decided that keeping her brain busy seemed the best way of distracting her senses. She dressed, braided her hair, ran downstairs and put on her coat. The clock ticked to 7.40 a.m.; twenty minutes until her shift. She didn't like cutting it so fine; she'd never been late. As she opened the door Aunt Kate met her at foot of the stairs.

'You're still looking a wee bit off colour. Are you sure you're up to work?'

Kate touched Layla's pale face. She did prefer to keep her in her sights but she had given her some freedom since it could help increase the speed of the process.

'I'll feel better when I'm busy.'

'Have a good day then, sweetheart.'

As she walked to the end of the path, Layla looked back. Aunt Kate watched her from the window, giving her a gentle wave but examining her with vigilant eyes. Layla had a strange feeling her Aunt Kate knew more than she was letting on.

Layla put on her iPod, though she had to lower the sound

somewhat. She took large but graceful strides toward the restaurant. She heard the tooting of a familiar car horn that seemed blend with her music. She slowed to a stop and a car drew up beside her. Ewan was in the driver's seat.

'Need a lift?' he called, having lowered the passenger window.

'I suppose you were going in my direction?' Layla said with a smile. She knew his game.

He smiled back and she jumped swiftly into the passenger seat.

'It's seems silly sitting here; I've not far to go. What are you doing out so early?' she said, raising her eyebrows.

He smiled but he did not answer. She didn't need to ask; she already knew the answer.

'Are you OK?' he asked.

There was concern written all over his face as he pulled up to the kerb outside the restaurant.

'You see,' she said, 'that was pointless. And yes, I'm fine!'

'I can't believe something like that could happen in the middle of the day. I don't know what this world's coming too. Duncan and I were oblivious. It was odd though because we were only a street away.'

She didn't want to talk about it any more; going to work had been a means of forgetting. She steered the subject away from herself. 'I haven't spoken to Megan. Do you know if she's OK?'

She remembered how Megan had given everything physically and mentally to save the man's life. She probably had as much idea as Layla that he had little chance of survival but she persisted and would not give up. The blood must have been turning her stomach inside out. Megan hated blood; she was the most stringent vegetarian Layla knew. A wounded animal usually upset her. She was sure Megan would be traumatised by the incident.

'I spoke to her mum. She's shaken up but she will be OK.

She's thinking of doing nursing or paramedics. Her mum said the police told them they thought it had been an accident. The evidence suggests he'd been so drunk he'd fallen on a broken bottle.'

'An accident?'

She tried to rein in her high-pitched voice.

'Well, there were certainly no witnesses to suggest otherwise,' he said.

Ewan had a matter-of-fact manner and no idea Layla was holding her breath. She nodded. An accident would be right for Megan's sake; it was wrong for her. She felt guilty and tormented, wondering if she had been the only witness or if an accident was the right explanation after all.

'Why are you always working, Layla?'

He was asking her questions which sounded trivial to her at that moment, but her mouth switched to automatic pilot, to cover her perplexing thoughts.

'Well, unlike you, Ewan, I don't have parents willing to pay my uni fees.'

'Ummm,' he grunted and then cleared his throat. 'Sorry, Layla, I don't know what I was thinking of.' His face reddened.

'Do you have high blood pressure, Ewan?'

He chuckled and gently shook his head.

'I know you better than that, Ewan. It's OK, really, and it's probably another reason why the death of a stranger doesn't hurt as much as losing the person you love most.'

She gave him a warm, comforting smile and once again masked her thoughts of being drawn to the gore.

'Layla, why are you comforting *me*?' He tilted his head, admiring her kind nature.

'I don't want you to feel bad.' If only he knew, she thought.

'Do you want to go out tonight? A peace offering, so I can ease my guilty conscience,' Ewan asked and then paused. 'I'll keep you safe!'

'I don't need protecting, Ewan!' She might need protecting from herself, though, she added silently to herself. An evening out might do her good, ground her. 'OK, I'll go but no overprotecting, and we're going as friends!'

Ewan smiled. She wasn't sure if that was him agreeing with her or humouring her.

'OK, I'll call for you at eight.'

She did think he sounded a little too pleased with himself. Was he rubbing his hands together? She'd give him the benefit of the doubt.

'Thanks for the lift,' she called as she ran into the restaurant, late.

Layla knew better than to give Ewan glimmers of hope; she felt selfish. He wanted more than friendship and she felt she'd encouraged him. She wished she could reciprocate his feelings but there wasn't a spark. He wore tinted glasses with her; he didn't see her darker side.

Layla and Leon busied themselves, washing floors, polishing glasses and cutlery. Or more to the point Layla busied herself; Leon pretended to look busy, and he was good at it. He had been hired when she took a little time off after her mother's funeral and they had spent a lot of time together. She confided in him when her mother died and he was always very concerned about her.

Layla had to keep reminding herself not to mention the incident she'd witnessed the previous day; Leon would have enjoyed the drama too much. She found herself staring at him, convinced he was on drugs. It had often crossed her mind when he indulged her in his stories of his hectic social life. She wondered if there was truth in any of his tales, but, since she hated small talk, it was far more bearable than general chitchat.

'You could come out for a bit of craic, as the Irish say,' Leon laughed.

His South African accent was not as brusque as others she

43

remembered. Her South African accent was now pretty much undetectable since she'd mastered a little of the Glaswegian twang. Leon was undoubtedly a South African but he didn't have any of the Bantu clicks or Afrikaans harshness in his voice. She found this unusual since she always remembered black Africans having more distinctive accents.

'I can't tonight. I'm afraid I'll have to take another rain check.'

He asked her to join him so often she was sure he thought she was avoiding his company.

'Don't worry. I was being polite. You don't seem to go out that much and you should.'

'I would go with you, honestly, but Ewan has already asked and I agreed to go out with him.'

She had no idea what Leon's intentions were, but then she was always somewhat naive when it came to male company. She was unnerved, too, by the thought of Leon making a pass at her.

'I'll hold you to that rain check!'

'You can. It rarely stops raining in this country,' she laughed.

They sat silent for a few minutes and then Leon spoke.

'Layla, I know it's none of my business ...' he began.

Layla giggled. Leon knew only too well why she was giggling but he ignored her and kept talking.

'I have these instincts about people,' he said. He paused.

'Go on!'

'Um,' he cleared his throat. 'I think Ewan has it bad for you. It's sort of obvious,' he said, playing the role of confidant.

Layla laughed. 'You don't say!'

'You know, how?' He silently congratulated himself on his role playing. He almost believed in it himself.

'Leon, do you think I was born in a bubble?'

She envied Leon's ability to communicate his emotions.

She wished she could be so in touch with herself and it reiterated how little she divulged to anyone. If she gave him any indication of her mindset he might freak. He went back into lecture mode.

'One on one might not be such a good idea. If you give him hope he'll only assume you're interested. It'll be more than a friendly night out for him. If I'm honest, you are leading him on a bit.'

Leon, always so direct! 'I know!'

She felt uncomfortable. Leon, however, saw innocence as opposed to discomfort.

'It's a bit of the girls can't be friends with boys and vice versa thing. You know, without something *more* developing. Females are pretty unpredictable. They can be seductive unintentionally. They can also be seductive and snare for their own gain.'

'What a load of codswallop,' she snapped.

Leon had never witnessed her being so verbal. It almost fascinated him. Had he hit a raw nerve?

'I'm friends with Duncan, too. And *you!*'

'OK, don't get your knickers in a twist,' he mocked.

'It's not a date!'

'Layla, you really are naive. I assure you; that's exactly what he thinks it is. Oh, and one other thing: Duncan *so* fancies you, too,' he said. Then he paused and gazed into her eyes and added, 'And you never know, maybe I have ulterior motives as well. I could be trying to get them out the way, so I can have you all to myself.'

Leon laughed loud.

Layla pursed her lips, amused.

'Duncan? Be serious! And as for you, no offence, Leon, but if you were the last man on earth I'd pass,' she laughed. Her body was shaking and she snorted with laughter.

'Nice,' he chuckled. He tried not to sneer. 'Layla, you've got to make your feelings clear ...' he whittled on.

45

Blah; blah; blah was all Layla could hear. She had stopped listening, but gave the odd nod to humour him.

Leon watched her intently; she was always deep in thought and keeping it to herself. She never gave too much away. He admired her beauty, and the fact that her appearance meant little to her. He thought it ironic she should be so eye-catching; she didn't fit a stereotype; she was unique. She was also very deep, though that wouldn't be a stranger's first perception. Each time Leon saw her she seemed to have morphed into an even more stunning being and she was still so young; he could not imagine how she would look with maturity. He had no doubt girls felt threatened by her, especially since men were drawn to her. This explained her small group of friends and her lack of trust in others.

To him, her eyes were her most telling feature. They often changed in hue, from olive-granite marbles to shiny green emeralds; they reflected her changeable moods. He noted how her eyes seemed to have remained predominantly dark since she had lost her mother. He had found it heart-wrenching keeping what he knew from her and he knew her emotions must have been terribly painful. Layla was looking at him with a deep frown, questioning his intentions. He knew she was mulling over his comments about keeping her for himself. The way he was looking at her, at that moment, admiring her, was probably adding to her confusion. He grinned; she was always so suspicious and presumed the worst.

Her head was tilted, feline-like, still studying him. Suddenly, she caught her reflection in his eyes and sat upright. The peculiar expression on his face was bemusing, especially when he laughed again.

'What's so funny?'

'I've been standing here thinking how funny we look together.'

'Why?' she giggled.

46

His laugh was so infectious.

'We're like a pint of Guinness: me, dark stout, and you, pale foam,' he said.

She nodded.

That evening, after her shift, when she was getting ready at home, she kept hearing Leon's warnings about Ewan's intentions. She wished she'd called the others to ask them to join them and when she dressed she made sure her outfit was understated. She felt quite shallow but she intended to keep his attention averted from her. She waited in the living room for him to arrive.

A loud doof-doof-doof rattled the front door. With a start she realised that it was Duncan's familiar knock. She darted to open it.

'How are …?' he began.

He couldn't finish; she'd thrown her arms around him.

'Layla, stop! You're choking me,' he said.

His voice was muffled.

'Oh Duncan … sorry; I didn't realise!'

'Aye … so I see …' He paused. 'Are you all right?'

He thought her warmth towards him strange; he usually irritated the life out of her.

'I didn't mean to jump at you. I'm just really pleased you're here.'

She stood back from the doorway to let him in. He raised his eyebrows and smiled.

'You look good, but you are a little pale and dark round the eyes. Are you sleeping?'

'I'm OK. I usually try to keep busy,' she said.

Layla ushered him into the living room; he tripped over the rug. She darted over to switch the lamp on.

'Saving electricity?' he chuckled.

'No.'

Another, more measured knock at the door interrupted the conversation.

'Ewan,' she said.

Her voice was a little high-pitched.

'We're going out tonight. Have you any plans? You could come with us.'

Duncan looked at her; he'd never seen her so unnerved and she seemed quite desperate for him to join them.

'Come on ... p*leeeease* ... It'll be fun.'

Other than getting on her hands and knees, there wasn't much else she could do, and he understood her predicament.

'I was going to watch a DVD and eat some popcorn and ice cream. I've actually invited me, myself and I to join me. I will say, they're great company,' he laughed.

'Obviously you're having a bit of a crunchy-nut-day,' Layla laughed.

She could sympathise; she'd been having one or two herself.

'Aye, with my imaginary friends I'm never lonely.'

Layla thought of her imaginary foes and how, if Duncan knew, he would definitely not have been very amused.

'I tell you what, Layla,' he said, 'I'll go along for Ewan's sake.'

He had a wicked sense of humour and she laughed, grateful he would be joining them.

'Thank you, thank you, thank you!' she said. She grabbed his face in her hands and kissed him, hard, on the cheek.

'Ow!' He flinched. She was freezing, but then her aunt's house was always cold.

Layla opened the front door. Duncan actually thought the temperature may have been as warm outside as in. He was distracted by Ewan's surprised face. He obviously had not expected to see both of them standing in the doorway. Duncan rubbed his cheek, removing Layla's lip gloss. A lengthy pause followed.

'Hello,' Ewan said.

He'd already noticed the shine on Duncan's cheek, and Layla knew immediately that he had misread the situation.

'Hi, Ewan,' she said, overenthusiastically as she tried to correct his conclusions.

'Duncan came round to see how I was,' she added.

Ewan remained mute. He nodded, but Layla ignored his displeasure. He could make all the assumptions he wanted; she had done nothing wrong.

Duncan was Ewan's most loyal friend and he was finding it even more uncomfortable. Layla noticed as she looked at them how they were standing in the shape of a triangle so she broke the shape.

Duncan had warned Ewan countless times about telling Layla about his feelings for her. Instead he waited. Duncan knew he feared her answer, it being quite obvious to all, including Ewan.

'Where to?' Duncan asked. He tried to lighten the atmosphere.

'I don't know,' Layla replied.

She turned to Ewan.

'Have you any ideas, Ewan?'

'A drink!'

Something told Duncan he had a table reservation to cancel. It was just as well he had agreed to go with them. Layla had enough complications to deal with and he felt Ewan's timing was questionable. Ewan had a habit of seeing something that wasn't there with girls; it had happened so many times in the past with other girls. Duncan took the opposite path. He'd watched his friends crash and burn romantically so many times and scare girls off; he had no intention of making the same mistakes himself.

'Not the city centre!' Layla insisted.

'No, of course not,' Ewan said as he nodded in agreement.

'Ugh; aye that's a good idea. You don't want to involve yourself in any more criminal activities,' Duncan teased.

He laughed and Layla giggled. Ewan stared dourly at them both.

'So, where to then?' she asked.

'We could go to Ashton Lane. There's always music on somewhere along there. Then after we could go with the fish and pishers to the chipper,' Duncan said with a laugh.

Layla was a little slow when it came to some of Duncan's jokes. She had no idea what he was talking about.

'What are fish and pishers?'

'I had a feeling you'd ask that; nothing goes by you,' Duncan chortled.

'You're a sarcastic git sometimes!' Layla said and rolled her eyes at him.

'Sorry, bonnie lass. I'm just a kidder. That's my dad's name for the drunk and disorderly folk who go to the chipper after a feed of drink. He reckons they don't wash their hands after a "pish" and end up eating fish and "pish".' Duncan roared with laughter.

Layla laughed along with Duncan and even Ewan couldn't contain his laughter for long either. He put his mood swing away for the night. He knew he would never win Layla over in one night anyway.

5

First Encounter

The university overlooked the concrete horizon of the city, paying homage to the industrial revolution. Apart from a bit of greenery below him, where a park followed the bank of the river for a few hundred meters, there were just buildings. Regan stood on the tarmac at the top of the hill and turned to face the entrance of the huge castle-like structure that was the university. It was oozing with Scottish heritage and as he walked through the open, solid-wood double doors he felt a sense of pride.

As he looked around the forecourt, he could hear an abundance of Scottish voices but there were many other accents, too. Some he could not place; some were distinctly English, French or Spanish. The students were all gathered on the lawns. Some of the faces looked so young he wondered how on earth they were students at the university. He also caught glimpses of a few 'mature' students; then again, he thought, they could just as easily be lecturers. He probably fitted into the 'mature' student category. He remembered Franky commenting on his age. If he remembered correctly his exact statement was along the lines of: 'Only twenty-two? You look like you've had a hard life!'

As he turned around in the middle of the lawn, taking in the entire structure, he thought how Harvard would probably have felt just as amazing had he been standing there on his first day. No thanks to the Scottish weather, he was filled with a warm and pleasurable feeling. He had never felt anything like it before. Something epic was stirring in his core and as he scanned the historic walls he thought of the wealth of heritage in Scotland and how the US was so young compared with it.

Regan noticed the different faculty doors. As he walked across the lawn he felt a little lost. He was alone. His two friends were not with him and, although he didn't mind being on his own, everyone seemed to be so deep in conversation. He wished for a moment that he had gone out with Kite and Franky on freshers' week and met one or two people. He put it to the back of his mind and walked toward a glass sliding door that looked somewhat out of place. The sign read 'Student Office' so he knew he was heading in the right direction.

Regan didn't expect to see much of Kite and Franky at classes. They were established students and they studied different courses. Although he would have enjoyed their company, another part of him was glad since he guessed they could have been rather distracting during lectures. They liked to socialise ... a lot, albeit mainly with each other. He noticed how they never really befriended anyone else, only him. They did respect his space and, although they invited him out on many occasions, they didn't push him to join them. Sometimes he wondered why they bothered with staying in halls at all, so rarely did they seem to be in it. It was just a place to sleep off hangovers.

When Regan reached the lecture hall he scanned the room for a seat. He felt a kind of awe as he thought about some of the previous students who had sat in that august room, illustrious people like Alexander Graham Bell. He sat third row up, on the fourth seat along. The room was filled with the scraping of chairs as the students took their places.

One thought, and the moment was ruined … his father! He wondered if those great men before him, like Bell, had had good and loving fathers, or if they had been as possessive and domineering as his father was. He had broken free from his grasp but not a day went by that he missed him. He never wanted to join the family business and his brother, Jimmy, had joined the Navy to escape that same fate. When Regan didn't enrol at Harvard his father had showed his disappointment – a degree from any other college was worthless in his eyes. Jimmy had always been his father's blue-eyed boy and Regan knew it, although he did think it funny, since Jimmy's eyes were actually green and his were blue. Regan knew he reminded his father of his mother too much; he looked like her, and he had her caring nature. He was just not ruthless enough to run the business successfully.

After lectures Regan walked around Kelvinside, familiarising himself with the area. He always liked to find his bearings in new places. He stopped at the Metro station, lifted a map and studied how large the whole of Glasgow was. For the time being he would keep to the west of the city, where he was residing. He'd been used to Bruges over the past few months, which was small and cosy. Although he was from Boston, he had never really ventured much away from his own suburb. Big cities unnerved him a little; he often questioned how he had found the courage to travel around Europe at all.

Regan turned off at the top of Byres Road. He stopped for a moment and laughed; only in Scotland could they have turned an old church into a pub. It was spilling over with life and he contemplated going in but the rumbling in his stomach was telling him he needed something with a little more substance than a pint. He noticed Kite and Franky on the steps trying to make their way in. They were obviously well intoxicated already and they never let him eat when they had gone out. He quickly turned the corner and walked briskly along Great Western Road. The long arterial road he walked had plenty of shops, banks and restaurants and he stopped to lift some cash from a cash point. He was ravenous, but most of the restaurants seemed shut. A small Italian café, with its lights on, caught his eye. He was sure he could eat the entire contents of a menu, but when he got to the door it was locked. He wanted to bang his head against the glass when he spotted two figures inside. He breathed with relief as he rapped on the door and a dark-haired, dark-skinned man walked over to the door. He was pointing aggressively to a sign hanging on the door. 'Closed' he read and put his head in his hands. A notice beside the door gave the opening time as 5 p.m. He looked at his watch: 2.40 p.m., over two hours away; he'd die from starvation in that time. He scanned the area hoping to find somewhere else open, and then he knocked again as the stern-faced man walked back toward the door. He looked as though he might eat Regan as he unlocked the door and peered out.

'We don't open until 5 p.m.,' he spat.

Regan's eyes widened.

'Yeah, sorry, I see that. I was just wondering if there's anywhere else open in the area.'

'Look man … we open in twenty minutes. We're not Tourist Information, you know. If you can't wait, go over the road and buy yourself a sandwich.'

'Twenty minutes? I thought you opened at five o'clock.' Regan looked at his watch.

'Five, that's what I said. Twenty minutes. However, by the time we finish this conversation it may well be closing time.'

'All right, there's no need for sarcasm, I don't know the area.' He realised that he had omitted to alter his watch to UK winter time.

'Like I said we're not …'

'Leon!'

A wind chime rang out from the back of the restaurant.

'For goodness' sake, don't be so rude. We're ready for customers. Let him in. The oven's nearly warm enough,' Layla said.

Leon glared at Layla.

She glared back. He liked a cup of coffee and a catch-up before service. In fact, he didn't like service at all. He wasn't the most hospitable of characters.

'Oh … all right,' he said.

He turned to the American freak. 'Well, come in then.' Bloody tourists, Leon thought.

'Thanks,' Regan said and gave a sincere and grateful nod, although Leon didn't deserve it.

'Where is it you want to sit?'

Leon played the extremely inconvenienced role well.

'Drink?' He took his order book from his pocket.

'Just a soda, thanks.'

Regan was a polite guy but had it not been for his hunger he would probably have walked out.

'Any particular one?'

'Cola … Coke,' Regan said.

Amazing, he thought, how one innocent word could be understood differently in different places in the world. He of course had met the masters of verbal communication. He thought he needed subtitles when he listened to his two leprechaun friends sometimes.

'What do you want to eat?'

Mr Happy was back with his soda. Regan hoped the waiter had another profession lined up since he must have been the worst waiter he'd ever met.

'Leon!'

Regan heard the female voice again. She walked into sight and instantly his hunger pangs disappeared. Instead the hunger he felt was not for food.

'I'll look at the menu first, thanks,' Regan replied.

He did not make eye contact with the waiter; his gaze was

transfixed on her. His eyes followed her as she moved. He'd never seen anyone so perfect, but more, he'd never imagined not being able to take his eyes off someone. So young, so beautiful, and there was something different about her, mysterious. She glanced at him and their eyes met, and something immediate happened, like a collision, the force enormous and unmistakable. They both bowed their heads, each feeling the intensity and the strange sensations. He forgot himself for a moment and stared openly; she did not break his gaze. Eventually he dropped his head to the floor as he remembered to feel embarrassed. He tried to distract himself from her and went to hang his coat over the back of the chair. As he moved the chair screeched along the floor and echoed through the silence. He wondered why he felt it necessary to screw his face up and close one eye. It certainly didn't reduce the noise.

'Ugh,' he grumbled.

As he scanned the room again, he tried to find a little composure. He was never usually so attracted to someone, especially if he didn't know them.

She couldn't helping looking at him again and noticed how he glowed in her vision with a warm aura. His eyes washed over her again. She noticed how blue his eyes were, like lagoons she could swim in. She did not recognise him and yet he seemed so familiar. She blinked and her sight changed from tunnel vision to what she took to be an optical illusion, as the details of his face seemed to move closer to her. She could see every mark including the scar above his right eyebrow. In a split second she had memorised all of his features in fine detail. She heard her mum saying: 'Remember, Layla, beauty is in the eye of the beholder.'

'Please, please, please, let me be the beholder.'

Leon was laughing and she realised she had said what she was thinking out loud. She hoped he hadn't heard. She glimpsed over again, but only briefly, as she tried to keep her gaze averted. His eyes had not faltered and they followed her as she moved. She could feel them boring into her back. She walked into the kitchen as she tried to make sense of how overwhelmed she was feeling. She could smell his scent, distinctive, not perfumed but intoxicating, and it drew her closer to him. She could have recognised his smell in a crowded room, even blindfolded.

Leon was standing in front of him, waiting to take his order. He'd lost his appetite, but he ordered anyway, realising it would prolong his time in the restaurant. Besides, she had been decent enough to let him in; the least he could do was order. He felt like a stalker. He had to prompt himself to inhale before he turned blue and he chuckled to himself. Since entering he had been every colour of the American flag except white. Although she added that white with her soft, milky skin. He remembered Kite and Franky's descriptions of the girls they encountered; surely she had to be the type of eye candy they so often shamelessly described. He could almost taste the sweet sensation of her on his lips; it felt strange.

Leon placed his order in front of him. It was a welcome distraction from his chain of thought. Kite and Franky were surely rubbing off on him as he seemed to be morphing into one of them. Wanton lust! He'd never imagined the mixed emotions and strange physicality it created; the feelings of pleasure and guilt, bitter-sweet and hard to ignore. He barely touched his meal. He could feel her watching him and he sensed a mutual connection between them. He always wondered how he would know if someone was attracted to him and he raised his head and smiled.

Leon was watching them; he'd never seen Layla reciprocate any emotion when a man showed interest in her and he found it intriguing.

Regan left with a heavy heart. He could not find the

courage to communicate with her verbally. Body language was foreign to him, he was not capable of being multilingual; he had no experience.

Regan raced back to halls looking for his cronies to distract him, although he most certainly was not going to tell them about her. They had no scruples about his feelings and could just as easily have fancied their own chances. He didn't want to take any risks.

Back at the restaurant Layla's heart fluttered; the angel of responsibility had definitely let her halo slip again. The past few months had been full of powerful emotion, exposing an appetite for at least four of the seven deadly sins that she never knew existed in her. Anger, lust, envy and pride; at least she wouldn't have to worry about gluttony with her recent loss of appetite. Where was it all leading. Is this what maturing meant?

Ugh, hormones! she cursed under her breath.

A magnetic field was pulling her toward a stranger and it worried her. Curiously it reminded her of the force that had drawn her toward the gore, and that had involved a stranger too. She was glad when her shift finished; she needed some air. She said goodnight to Leon and left; she hadn't spoken to him much throughout the shift, and she felt thankful the restaurant had been busy.

Layla had the house to herself for the evening; a bonus, since it would mean no probing from her aunt. She was certain Aunt Kate would have sensed her unease; she usually did. Her eyes usually gave her mood away anyway. She lay on her bed and stared into the mirror. She could see every detail of them and they were dark. She tried to change them as she chose to, instead of by her mood. Hours passed but she refused to give up until she had the ability to hide her feelings behind her changeable eyes. The darkness in her room seemed to help her focus better and she eventually found a technique that worked, although it was going to take time to master.

Her eyes began to water and with the tears she felt relief. She was crying; it had been impossible before. When she looked down she could see the tears were deep-red blood. At first she thought she'd cut herself; she didn't think she was crying after all though she could feel the emotion. As she lay on her saturated pillow, the release seemed to give her a little clarity and she pulled a tissue from a small box on her bedside cabinet and dabbed the blood away. Suddenly the intense feeling began to fade; the pain changed to a dull ache.

Morning came and Layla danced down to the kitchen, whistling. Her aunt's eyes were wide as she watched her, bewildered.

'Amazing ... have you been at the sugar again?'

Layla just smiled.

'A revelation,' her aunt said.

'Yeah ... a real eye-opener,' she said.

Aunt Kate smiled. She really didn't seem that far from maturity now. She noticed how much clearer her eyes seemed. Everything was going nicely to plan. She had coordinated everything perfectly and Layla had no idea.

'So, have you any plans today?'

'Work ... unfortunately.'

'That's the first time I've ever heard you say unfortunately about work; you're usually a workaholic,' Kate said.

Layla tried out her new technique with her eyes. 'Oh I just feel a lot happier all of a sudden,' she explained blithely.

'You look radiant, Layla. I don't think I've ever seen you looking so relaxed.'

Layla giggled, but, although she did feel better, she was more pleased that she was giving her aunt no idea of her mindset.

'Happy days,' Layla said (and she meant it).

'Aye, you're right, happy days, Layla.' (Kate meant it too.)

As her eyes reflected what she wanted them to, Layla's mood lifted further.

'OK, I'm off. Have a nice day.' She blew her aunt a kiss.

'OK … bye.'

Aunt Kate was delighted that Layla was feeling calm; after all the storm was ahead.

Layla had a feeling the American would return and, sure enough, he didn't even wait until evening service. She scanned him and watched as he furrowed his brow, imagining running her fingers over the creases on his forehead and smoothing them away. An aroma tickled her throat, a familiar feeling but one she had learned to ignore; attraction was a strange feeling for her. His heart pumped in her ears louder than her own and she choked at the thought of the liquid pulsating through his veins. The lust and desire sent her all-a-quiver.

'Hi,' he said.

Layla turned to the counter. She panicked as he stood before her, feeling slightly dishevelled, and she straightened her clothes to disguise her obvious feelings; a clever, but common female diversion.

'Hello,' she replied.

'I wanted to thank you for letting me in early yesterday,' he gulped.

'Oh, that's fine; it was freezing out there.' They were both nervous.

'I'm Regan,' he said.

He extended his hand.

'It's nice to meet you,' she said.

She took his hand in hers. Her throat ached; dry as a bone.

'Wow, you're right. It *is* cold; your hand's icy!' Regan said.

Layla couldn't hear the words, only the deep American

accent, and then, as she registered what he said, she pulled her hand away and wiped it on her apron.

'Oh, my hands are always cold.'

'Cold hands, warm heart,' he said.

He blushed and she smiled to save his discomfort.

'You're not from around here, are you?'

'Well, I am now,' she said.

He smiled. 'Yeah, and I'm from around he-ah,' he said with a raspy American accent, dropping his *r*s.

'You have the strangest Glaswegian accent I've ever heard,' she giggled.

He laughed.

'I'm American,' he said.

'I guessed.'

He laughed again, realising how awkward and rudimentary his attempts at conversation were.

'Do you mind if I order? I'm in a bit of a hurry; I have lectures,' he said.

'Yes, no problem,' she said, 'I'll bring it over.'

He made her think about her plans for university. She had postponed her enrolment while she grieved for her mother. She noted how he looked a little older than her.

'Thanks,' he said. 'I'm Regan by the way,' he repeated, and then realised his mistake. He flushed pink. Layla found his innocence endearing and she poured the Coke and handed it to him.

'Here you go,' she said warmly. 'I'm Layla.'

He smiled as he realised that he might not have scared her off after all.

Layla busied herself while his eyes followed her, just as they had the previous day, and she liked it. Leon gave Regan his order as she occupied herself with the rush. Lunchtime specials, courtesy of the proprietor, attracted countless students, and since Leon spent most of his time flustered, Layla usually had to pick up the bulk of the work. Leon still found it necessary to spend most of his time moaning about the workload; it was perpetual.

The customers had a tendency to leave at the same time so Layla had almost forgotten about the American until he set his bill on the counter and asked to pay. He took deep breaths as she placed his change in his hand and he put it into the tip jar. She smiled.

'I'm going away for a few days,' he said. 'I wasn't supposed to be going for another month but my friends brought it forward.'

He was revealing a lot of unnecessary information; she just assumed he was nervous. He cleared his throat, knowing how he waffled endlessly, but she was patient.

'Want to catch a movie sometime? Maybe when I get back?'

Layla hated cinemas – the volume screeched in her ears – but she was attracted to him, so it was a no-brainer. Infatuation was uncharacteristic for her but she fancied the dark-haired, blue-eyed American and she would agree to the movie. He waited, wondering when she would blow him out. Ugh, when would he get a bit more ... *gusto* for such things!

'Yeah, OK!'

He wasn't expecting it.

'Really?' he screeched; surprised. 'Really?' he repeated with slightly more confidence in his voice.

'Yes,' she said.

'I'll ring you when I get back?'

'I'm free tonight.' She surprised herself.

Gusto, he thought.

'Great,' he said.

He wanted to whoop, but refrained.

'I'll meet you outside the Metro station at eight.'

Her new skill, hiding her mood behind her eyes, meant he had no idea how eager she was, whereas normally they would have stood out on stalks.

She watched as he left the restaurant and bumped into two

friends. Her heart began to pump in her chest. The murderer was real and he was with the American. She could hear his voice. He didn't *sound* demonic, but he was; she'd seen the evidence. He'd not been a figment of her imagination; she *had* seen him hiding in the dark. The American called him Franky and when he laughed, shivers rolled up her spine. In her mind she screamed and she turned and fled to the kitchen. She felt pure fear and she could not stop trembling. She wondered if a naked eye would notice her body rattling from inside. Leon went into the kitchen.

'Hi, I feel like ... Layla ... what's wrong? You look faint. Here ... wait.'

He ran into the restaurant, grabbed a chair and carried it back into the kitchen.

'Sit! Sit!' he insisted.

She didn't respond.

'Sit down, Layla!' He raised his voice still more. 'Would you listen to me? Sit down!'

He helped her to the chair and poured a glass of water.

'Layla, drink this!'

He soaked a dishcloth and dabbed her wrists and forehead. He rinsed it out and wiped the sweat beads from her face.

'Layla, I'm going to call a doctor.'

'No! ... No doctors,' she bellowed.

'OK, OK, calm down, no doctors! Just tell me what happened!'

She took slow, deep breaths.

'I don't feel well.'

He looked at her confused.

'You were in great form a moment ago. What happened?'

He didn't believe her. She seemed shaken, not ill.

'It just came over me,' she cried.

Tears rolled down her cheeks, bloody and red, and she covered her face with her cloth to hide them.

Leon's stomach somersaulted. Layla didn't cry.

'I'm going to ring your aunt!'

'No,' she snapped, 'I'll be fine.'

It was peculiar, tetchy behaviour and he detected anger in her voice. He'd never seen her so unstable, even though he had long been expecting the phase he was witnessing. Despite her protests he phoned her aunt and, as he expected, she didn't sound surprised.

Kate arrived outside the restaurant and waited behind the tinted glass of her Mercedes.

Layla ran to the car and Kate drove her home. She saw in a moment that something in Layla had changed, but something had definitely instigated the transformation. Realisation usually came with maturity but something had quickened the change.

Layla went to her room. She needed to focus; she avoided speaking to her aunt for fear she wouldn't allow her to meet Regan. Layla needed to find out if Regan had been involved in the killing.

She got herself ready with mixed emotions … fear and excitement. Through it all she couldn't help the attraction she still felt for Regan. She was unsure if it was he or the gore pulling her to him; she had felt that before too.

He was waiting for her outside the Metro station. With each step she could feel him enticing her and she forced herself to focus more clearly. He agreed to go for a coffee instead of the cinema; it meant she could probe him for information. They ordered a coffee and started with small talk. Layla hated small talk, now even more than usual, but she had his trust to gain. She started her investigations.

'Have you made many friends?' she said.

'No. Not really. I have two Irish friends I met while travelling,' he said.

He seemed to give up the information about his friends

very willingly, which she found strange. Surely someone involved in such an awful deed would have concealed it.

'You didn't meet them here?' she went on.

He felt a little confused by her tone and noticed how dark her eyes seemed in the dim light. She blinked, sensing his suspicions. 'No, I met them in Bruges. We all worked in a pub over last summer.'

Her questions amused him. She seemed to be scoping him out, and he found it intriguing, at first.

'So have you been into the city yet?'

'No, I'm behind in my coursework. I started late in the semester so I have to catch up.' She sighed under her breath. He hadn't even been into the city, but his friend had and she hadn't been hallucinating at all.

'Where are you from, Layla? You don't *sound* very local.'

She wondered how she should answer.

'Here and there; we travelled a lot when I was a child,' she said.

She smiled, trying to melt the ice a little. He did seem really easy to talk to since she never normally answered anything directly. She barely gave her aunt straight answers and found it odd that she was being so receptive to a stranger especially someone she'd thought of as consorting with a murderer.

'Was your father in the armed forces?'

'No, not exactly, it was my mum's work. What about you? What brought you here?'

'Fate maybe,' he smiled.

Everything was moving very quickly but Layla liked it; she couldn't do with beating about the bush.

'Where are your friends tonight?'

'Oh they've gone to feed themselves. I'm meeting them in the morning.'

Layla's eyes darted and then opened wide. What a peculiar turn of phrase! Feed themselves!

'You didn't mention you were going with them on your trip,' she said.

'No, I know. I didn't realise it was relevant. Don't tell me you're one of those possessive bunny boilers!' He laughed to lighten the mood.

'No. I just wondered how well you know them.'

The atmosphere felt a little tense again. 'Pretty well, they have been like brothers to me and since I lost my own brother a few years back they are the closest I have to family.'

He really did give her a lot of personal information freely. He seemed too open to be heartless but she was concerned about him, about his safety.

'Oh sorry, I didn't mean to pry.'

It felt good to tell someone about his brother and he was not normally so forthcoming with personal information. It surprised him how openly he spoke to her.

'I could do with some fresh air,' he said, 'do want to take a walk through the Botanic Gardens?'

She lifted her coat, not that she felt the cold much, but everyone wore a coat in Scotland and it seemed appropriate. She remembered telling her mother she couldn't acclimatise when in reality the weather hadn't affected her in an age.

'Sure, it is a bit stuffy in here.'

They walked along toward the Botanic Gardens but it was closed, so they wandered along Byers Road.

'Would you like to go in for a drink?'

'I'd love to but I have any early shift in the morning; I'm going to have to get home.' She needed time to think and, if, when he came back, she still felt drawn to him, that was when she'd do something about it. For the moment she needed to concentrate on bringing a killer to justice.

'Will your friends be coming back with you, particularly the Franky one?'

Her final question, but he seemed a bit narked. He'd spent

most of the night answering questions about his two Irish friends and he wondered whom she was more interested in. Everyone seemed to ask a lot about Franky. He was finding him a bit of a weasel at that point in time; he felt a little jealous so he didn't answer. She didn't ask again, having sensed his annoyance.

He walked her to her door.

'I would invite you in but my aunt's a bit strange.'

'No it's OK; I have an early start.'

'Is everything all right?' she asked.

'Yeah … fine!'

'You're not jealous, are you?'

She was a little shocked, but she could see why he would perceive she was interested in his friend.

'Um … no!'

She giggled.

'Oh no; you are! Let me assure you I have no romantic interests in either of your friends. I'm sorry if I made it seem that way. I'm just really nosy,' she said.

'No, I'm sorry; it was pretty childish.'

He leaned over to kiss her forehead.

'You're freezing! Go in and get warm,' he said and rubbed her shoulder. She let him, although it made little difference to her body temperature.

'Thanks. Listen, Regan, please be careful; I'd really like to see you again, although you may want to run after this date. I'm just full on.'

She smiled, hoping she hadn't scared him off. She'd added two and two and come up with five, but the friend needed investigating for sure.

'Layla, can I kiss you?'

'One minute I'm a bunny boiler and now you want to kiss me. Hmm, let me think.'

She paused, letting him think she really wasn't sure if she wanted him to kiss her. Instead she took the initiative and forcefully pulled him to her. The kiss was intense, not like she ever imagined a first kiss to be. It felt very physical but also emotional and he reciprocated the emotion. She put her arms around his neck and he pulled her closer. He could feel every inch of her form and the ache in his groin was stronger than ever. She could feel his arousal and could barely pull herself away from him. She didn't want him to get the wrong idea about her, although she could quite easily have thrown herself at him. He pulled her away from him. He wanted to preserve the feelings he had for her. He wanted it to last a lot longer than any of Franky's or Kite's conquests. It felt good but he had to show some control. As he pulled away from her, she nicked his lip.

'I'm so sorry!'

She was embarrassed but he loved it; the pain of the passion turned him on.

'Good night, Layla. Thank you for a lovely evening. I can't wait to see you again.'

He had turned himself away slightly, not wanting to expose what could easily be seen. 'Ring me when you get back. Oh yeah ... your telephone number might be good ...'

She gave him her number and turned to let herself in. Before he ran off, he pulled her to him and gently kissed her, then turned and ran back to his halls.

She could taste his blood on her lips; it was intoxicating. She felt slightly drunk as she memorised every detail of their kiss.

Night became morning quicker than it had ever before, and every night after that she fantasised about Regan as she imagined him taking her in every sense of the word. It felt as though the physical passion alleviated her frustrations and had he been back in halls she would have been round there in a flash.

Oh Layla, Layla, you bad girl, she thought. She'd never been bad but she liked it.

She didn't like the company Regan kept and she intended to make short of them, or at least Franky.

He texted her every hour. She couldn't wait for her phone to beep and she couldn't wait for them to meet again and from what he said neither could he. But the days dragged on and he did not return.

6

Conception

Kate lifted Marie's diary. Such a lot of detail, she thought, as she read it.

February 1982
Flashes of lightning illuminates the sky but the thunder doesn't rumble, it explodes! The wind is sweeping rain over the vineyards on the Stellenbosch hills, watering the vines that produce some of the finest wines in the world.

The Copper Can acquires all its produce in the local area, including the wine and venison it serves. The sterling reputation brings diners from near and far to sample the cuisine. I've managed the restaurant now for almost two years. The restaurant's popularity means tables usually have to be reserved in advance.

'I had to double our orders this week,' I said to him, and he nodded in acknowledgment.

'The vineyard said they'd deliver by Thursday and I'll get the perishables from the wholesalers Friday morning,' I added.

'I'll get the venison. Will it take double?' Connor offered, as he always did.

'Yeah … definitely; both sittings are fully booked.'

Amara Demarco owns the restaurant and I have little time

for her. She lives like a hermit, rarely showing her face in daylight, but she pays well and never interferes in the day-to-day running so I tolerate her. Connor lives with Amara. She has a commune in the hills of Gordon's Bay. The bay area is picturesque, and exclusive (evident in the expensive yachts docked at the pier). It houses her magnificent property, an old-style Cape Dutch house hidden among a plantation of trees. She dresses like a hippie and acts like a hippie, and the free-love stuff suits her well. I, thankfully, do not have many dealings with her, but when I do I prefer the meetings to take place in the restaurant. All the male staff live in Amara's commune and claim she charges nominal rent. I often wonder if it's more a case of payment in kind. She often fusses about the female staff, and I assume it is more a case of jealousy, although I do notice that the males tend to be more reliable. Many of the females don't return after a few shifts. Stellenbosch, being a university town, has an abundance of students seeking part-time work, so replacements are never a problem.

Connor is assistant manager; he practically lives in the restaurant and is more than capable of running it. Sometimes I wonder why Amara even employed me.

My relationship with Connor developed into a firm friendship. I have always been wary of men, but Connor seems even more wary of me, initially. I've been in a disastrous long-term relationship with a bit of control freak so I tend to avoid male company. Connor is different! He spends time unravelling my thoughts and my feelings.

I am the opposite of Amara, in looks and personality. I am fair with green eyes and, I hope, a warm personality. I take Connor at face value and he seems to like my warmth. Amara is striking and mysterious, with mahogany hair, coffee skin and cold, dark eyes. She is a seductress.

Connor is pasty, cold and unsociable but I saw the light in him and he's started to emerge from the shadows. We spend nights locked in conversation after closing. He has an unusual accent with a mixture of Irish tones, that I find almost as difficult as him to unravel. My accent is distinctly Irish.

April 1982
Last night Connor and I really opened upto each other. I told him stuff I've told no one else.

'I left Ireland with my twin sister before I was seventeen. My mum sort of threw us out!' I told him when he probed about my past. I had never opened up so easily. 'Kate and I never made any contact with her. We were both angry. And then a few days after our seventeenth birthday it was ...'

I cleared my throat, my eyes burned, but I refused to show any emotion.

'Um ... it was too late!'

He listened as though he felt my sadness.

'Anyway, my sister lives in Glasgow. She married an Irishman, someone from home; she sort of followed him. He is a lot older than her, but hey, we have no one to disapprove. And I was in a relationship but it didn't work out ... so now I roam!'

I smiled.

I felt so much contentment in Stellenbosch and, other than Kate, I had no reason to return to the northern hemisphere. I hadn't felt at home in such a long time. I wondered if Connor had something to do with that, since I thought about him day and night. I had butterflies in my stomach every time I saw him or every time I thought about him. Sometimes they fluttered so much it made me queasy. I would go into work knowing he was there, and it pleased me.

'How long have you lived with Amara?' I asked. It was an intrusive question.

He didn't like small talk, but he never revealed much about his private life.

'A while,' he answered.

It seemed he knew everything about me and I could barely get past his front cover. I did notice how much brighter his eyes seemed, than when we first met.

'Marie,' he said.

He put his hand on mine and gently grasped my lean fingers. My heart skipped a beat. His hand felt cool, with a unique texture and I never wanted him to let go. It was as though he knew it would lead to some kind of pain and yet he seemed powerless to the emotion. He leaned forward slowly, carefully and placed his lips on mine. I was shell-shocked, but responded with intent. I could not get beyond his eyes even though they were looking into mine. I could only see as deep as he allowed, so I closed my eyes as our tongues fused. He walked me to my car never letting go of my fingers. I rolled down the window; he leant in and kissed me again. We never spoke. I was very distracted and I had to slam the brakes as he stepped in front of the car.

'You left your handbag on the roof,' he smiled.

I blushed and giggled.

This morning when I woke the sun shone through my window and, although it sat low in the sky, I knew it was early. I could hear ringing in the background. I thought I'd been dreaming, but when it rang again I knew it was the phone. I wondered who it could be. It was my day off and the restaurant was closed.

I was still groggy when I answered the phone but that did not alter my elation when he spoke.

'Do you remember what happened last night?' he asked.

'Yes, it's a bit hard to forget,' I said.

'Could we meet at the restaurant at dusk?'

I should have gone with my instinct and rejected his invitation, but because I couldn't wait to see him again, I accepted.

'Marie, I don't think you'll like what I have to say,' he said as we sat in the restaurant garden in the last rays of the sun.

'Well, I'm not sorry,' I replied.

'I think we made a mistake. I have to be with Amara. I don't know what I was thinking,' he said.

I wanted to cry; I realise now I've loved him a long time, long before he kissed me. But I would never have initiated physical contact with him because of Amara. I simply forgot all my principles; in fact I binned them. A pain shot through me, but I never wanted him to think something so trivial as a kiss could cut so deeply.

'I know you live with her. I didn't expect undying love; it was only a kiss,' I said.

It felt like a knife twisting inside me, it was never about the kiss. I wound a piece of hair tighter and tighter around my finger, reminding myself not to let go of my emotions.

He nodded.

'I should go,' I said.

I had to leave. He reached out to touch me but I shrugged him off. I wanted to speak and even went as far as opening my mouth but nothing came out. Then the words rolled from my tongue; perhaps it was spite.

'I don't care if you don't like what I have to say. She's bad for you but obviously you're blinded. I've been a fool and I think you know why. You should never have acted as you did if you didn't feel the same way.'

At that, I turned, lowered my head and left. He took a few steps behind me but then he stopped. I could feel his confusion and torment.

July 1982

I love him too much to discard the friendship. If that is all he can offer I have decided to take it, rather than nothing, so I've kept my position at the restaurant, and stifled my feelings. I suspect Amara has sensed the sentiment between us because she took great pleasure in marking her territory. Suddenly she's begun to visit the restaurant more often and throws herself at him at every opportunity. He responds, and they flaunt their desires, but still I ignore them. I am wounded but I refuse to let my guard down and give her any satisfaction. I've made an effort to meet new friends, and have started socialising to divert my attentions away from Connor. Amara is often at the places I go to, and when he wasn't with her, she fawns over other men. The other three staff members are usually involved with her in some way too.

One night a couple of weeks ago after work I went, with a couple of my new friends, dancing. This kind of nightlife suits me, since work often runs on into the late hours. I never see Connor socially; we don't even talk about anything other than work-related matters.

Amara and the rest of her commune, bar Connor, were there that night. She was dancing with a handsome stranger. I wished I could be so bold but she has a relationship I would give anything for and I was incensed by her obliviousness to Connor's feelings. I dream of being loved so absolutely by someone that special. I couldn't help but stare at Amara's brazen, hussy-like conduct, which became hotter, and heavier, and left little to the imagination. How can Connor be so committed to a fraud? I was thinking. One of the waiters, a house mate of Connor's was standing beside me.

'She's unreal, isn't she?'

I turned to face him. 'Will you tell Connor?'

He looked at me baffled.

'Why would I do that?'

I thought I'd misheard. 'Because he has no idea what she's like.'

He looked at me; his facial expression spoke volumes. It asked if I was some kind of idiot. It only confirmed to me that Connor already knew all about Amara, and chooses to ignore it.

'So she can make a fool of him and you would say nothing,' I said.

'What are you talking about, Marie?'

'I'm talking about how she openly cavorts with other men and no one seems to think there's anything wrong.'

I became annoyed as he sniggered under his breath.

'It's nothing to do with me.'

'Nice!'

I turned and marched out. I knew I couldn't tell Connor myself. He would think it spite and it would have killed our friendship, but I felt very guilty.

I ran through home in torrential rain. Thunder rolled and lightning lit up the night starless sky. As I passed the restaurant I noticed the lights on and I could see Connor's silhouette and I knew I had to tell him. Friends told each other everything regardless of their own gain. His eyes fixed with mine as I walked toward him; dripping wet. My clothes clung to me, and I pulled my wet hair away from my face. He listened when I told him, but he did not react. I thought he must have liked the challenge. It was probably why he was not interested in me. He walked over to me, put his hands on my shoulders and then took me in his arms. He kissed me; he seemed hesitant, like he would break me, and then he loved me as though I were a china doll. I could barely contain my own passion and in the heat of the moment became almost obsessive. It was as though our souls had merged. That night was enough for me, for ever.

September 1982
Another month has passed since I last wrote here. Something else has happened, something

The grandfather clock in the corner of the room had just chimed 4 p.m. We chopped, diced and marinated; polished and gleamed and prepared for service.

'Everything is running so smoothly,' I said.

He nodded but remained silent. He seemed deep in thought …

Kate stopped reading thinking how Connor had almost certainly realised by this point who Marie was. It had probably never occurred to him, before then, that her sister had married his best friend, John. He knew about the punishment John's vamp had inflicted on him when she found him. Kate remembered him being a witness to the execution, along with the other members of the covens. He had also witnessed Briege change her, for being his wife, to ensure she suffered an eternity of torment. Kate almost felt his angst as she realised his intentions were to save Marie from the same fate. Kate knew about Amara, too; she'd been involved in John's execution, too. In fact, she was on her list. Kate opened the diary again.

As the night went on I sent the rest of the staff home.
'Are you sure you don't want me to stay on, Marie. There's still plenty to do?' the young waiter offered. I remember his boyish features. He didn't live with Amara, but then she had not been introduced to him at that stage.

'No, it'll be fine. Connor and I don't mind finishing up,' I said, winking at Connor. He usually knew what that meant, but this time he shuffled uncomfortably.

'They look like they're here for the night; maybe we should get them some sleeping bags,' I chuckled.

Connor nodded but he did not seem to have his sense of humour with him.

'I was just agreeing with you,' he said.

I marched to the kitchen. How did he always know what I was thinking? I could feel him watching me so I went back to the dining room to clear some of the empty tables. Connor cleared the bar and, although I tried to ignore him, he kept staring at me.

At last the customers were leaving.

'Thanksh ... for a great ni ... ght um ... mm ... meal. You're rrrrrrep, ugh, it was good,' the burly man said,

77

slurring his words, barely able to complete his sentence.

'No, thank you,' I said. I didn't really mean it, I was glad to see the back of them. It really didn't matter since he was too drunk to notice.

'I'm not dink ... I'm not dunk .... um ... shorry!'

'Thank you so much,' a lady said, 'I didn't sample as much wine as my friend here. The food was superb.'

I bid them goodnight.

'Goodnight,' the five said together; some with more sobriety than others.

Connor locked the door behind them and as he turned I noticed how his milky face soured with each step he took toward me. I lowered my eyes trying not to make eye contact; I already saw the dismay on his face. I raised my gaze and his solemn eyes apologised. I knew everything I needed to in the confinement of that silence. My Irish four-leaf clover, from that moment, lost a leaf.

'I'm sorry,' he said.

'I'm not,' I scolded.

I sprinted as fast as my feet would carry me.

He walked a few paces. I could hear him, but then he stopped ...

Kate stopped reading for a moment. She didn't usually feel any emotion, but even she felt how heart-wrenching the story was. He must have let her go to protect her. The only way was to let her believe he didn't want her, before she discovered the truth about him, or she surely would have taken her chances to be with him just as she had with John. Kate sensed his pain and as she thought of his sacrifice a single bloody tear rolled down her cheek.

I knew I lost him that night. The finality in his eyes meant there would be little point in fighting for him. I packed what I could; returned to the car, and drove away. I drove for hours before I pulled in. I put my head over the steering wheel and sobbed, uncontrollably. I did plan to tell him about the baby that night; it was meant to be a celebration, not the end. It was then I found an envelope and a small jewellery box in my pocket. In the box was a necklace. The note read:

Marie,
The necklace was my mother's, the only other woman I ever loved. I am truly sorry.
My tormented soul will love you always,
Connor.

Kate closed the book; the rest was history. Layla had told her how her mother used to cry herself to sleep, but Marie had never mentioned it.

7

Initiation

Glenarm was the first of the Nine Glens of Antrim. The Glens were world-renowned for their scenery and were a wonder of the natural world.

The serene, charming village lay on the north-east coast of Ireland and was home to Franky and Kite. They had warned Regan not to use the Americanism 'quaint' when referring to the village. They assured him, if he did, it would be his last word. They claimed the American tourists used the word so often it had become a dirty word to them and that made Regan laugh.

Franky and Kite, they said, were staying in their tiny family homes; they were too small for him too, so he had taken up residence in a narrow, three-storeyed house with a range in the kitchen and an outside toilet; it was quaint, although he didn't say so. It did have a bathroom inside, but the mere idea of an outside one fascinated him. It was both a B&B and a home; it had belonged to the owner's family for generations and had been passed from father to oldest son, in the Irish country tradition. The village consisted of only one or two roads, but it had quite a few pubs and a corner shop owned by locals. An old grey castle guarded the entrance to the village, which was surrounded by forest on three sides and by the sea on the other. He couldn't imagine his friends living somewhere so small, and yet he got the distinct impression they wanted to settle back in. He did envy them in some way; he didn't know where he would end up, although he hoped it involved Layla in some form.

The landlady made Regan breakfast. Kite sat at the table with him and she set it in front of Regan.

'Kite, I've never seen so much food on one plate! Is this all for me?'

Kite laughed. 'That's just for starters! It's the Irish way; you can't stay here and not be fed,' Kite said matter-of-factly.

'I can't remember the last time anyone cooked for me,' he said.

'You look like you could do with a good feed; you're wasting away. The landlady thought it was the booze,' Kite added with a laugh.

Franky walked in.

'So are we going to Hunters tonight?' he said almost without a good morning. 'Come on, Yankee Sullivan, what do you say to a night out? It's the time to go forth and conquer. Come on, I'm not taking no for an answer.'

Franky kept on badgering him; he knew he wouldn't give up until he agreed. He didn't really need much persuading since it would help refocus his mind a little and distract him from his thoughts of Layla for a while. He knew without doubt that the evening would include his friends' customary efforts of trying to add a notch to their bedposts. The pub they would be going to could not have a more fitting name for Kite and Franky; they liked nothing more than preying on young girls … well, any girls actually. Watching them crash and burn always entertained him and he chuckled to himself.

'You're driving. Neither of us has a car and sure you don't drink anyway.'

Kite always seemed so commanding.

'Yeah … sure, no problem,' Regan said.

81

Kite forgot to tell him a couple of other people would be hitching a lift but he knew Regan would agree.

'Regan, I've organised a game of five-a-side football … Oops, I mean soccer … Are you up for it?' Franky asked.

'Yeah should be good. Are you going, Kite?' Regan asked.

Kite claimed to have pulled a muscle in his leg.

'I was going to rest it,' Kite said, suddenly rubbing it enthusiastically. 'Hopefully it'll get a little light exercise tonight,' he said.

He winked and tilted his head skyward, and then laughed outrageously.

'Do you think of anything else? Is there anyone you wouldn't try it on with?' Regan joked. He was quite certain he already knew the answer.

'Franky's sisters,' Kite replied.

'I didn't know Franky *had* sisters,' Regan said.

'I don't … Kite's being smart,' Franky fumed.

Later that day, at dusk, Regan went for a walk along the seafront. It reminded him of his brother. He shivered at the thought of him slowly freezing to death in the iron-dark Irish Sea. He remembered their close relationship, and how his family had fallen to pieces after his death. He'd only been in the Navy a few years. Girls were Regan's subconscious link to his brother. Jimmy loved the fairer sex, and relished love's alluring magic. Regan had spent his time avoiding girls; he didn't believe he had Jimmy's charm. Then he met Layla, and it had all happened so naturally. He hoped when he returned it would be just as magical.

Kite and Franky were always surprised by Regan when he did go out with them. His modesty seemed to create a magnetic field around him. He was never without attention. They suspected his inexperience was as apparent to girls as to them, and he was oblivious. He always declined female offers; he seemed to be waiting for something more. Kite could see Regan shunned the 'try before you buy' policy they had. He found it intriguing, but realised it could not be mimicked, at least not by him.

A little distance away Colleen Duffy lingered in the trees, watching him. Every minuscule detail always became clearer as evening loomed and she would be able to venture outdoors. She took great care to observe all the characteristics of potential mates. Here was a tourist in the area for a short time, someone unknown to locals; it was perfect. She noticed his reserved mood. That usually quickened the change. She detected a distinct lack of confidence too; that was an added bonus. This was a rare characteristic and made for easy coven management. She hoped his human traits stayed with him after transformation; she could keep him or trade him and that would make the change worth it. His virtue made him incredibly valuable, such mates were few and far between. Her mouth watered; she could smell the blood coursing through his veins, the virgin blood. It was stronger and more alluring than any other, which meant she had to take care.

Regan walked across the road to the football pitch and met with the other players beneath the massive castle walls. Franky introduced Regan to the other locals. Kite didn't play; he could not contain his strength. Franky had the power to restrain himself in that way.

'Does anyone live in there?' Regan asked as he turned to one of the players.

'Yeah … a fit woman, and her brothers. Kite and Franky could tell you better; they know them,' the player answered.

Franky appeared from nowhere.

'Regan and I are going out with Kite tonight. Regan's the designated driver. We finally found a friend with transport!' Franky said.

'Franky, you're mad; nights out with you usually end with someone getting hurt,' the player said, looking at Regan.

The team-mate's remark, meant as a joke, was all too often

true; Franky didn't seem to have any self-restraint when he was drinking.

'You're on side,' Franky shouted.

The other player dribbled for goal, but missed.

'You couldn't score a slate,' Franky shouted. He didn't like losing.

'Franky, you're running in the wrong direction,' Regan jibed.

Franky slotted the ball in the back of the net and celebrated like an acrobat. Regan stared, stunned. The Irishmen were never done surprising him and he laughed loudly. Regan enjoyed the match and meeting the rest of the players. They had the same dry sense of humour as Kite and Franky. He even scored himself.

'So ... you scored,' Franky said after the match.

'Yeah, I have played before. Don't seem so surprised.'

Franky laughed. 'Regan, you *never* score!'

'I think you'll find I have scored, with someone you could only dream of.'

Franky pondered Regan's words; he and Kite had brought their trip forward for that very reason. They feared he would gain too much experience and therefore be devalued and that would have posed serious problems for them.

'Well ... Kite's going, so I can't imagine there'll be any scoring tonight either,' Regan said.

Everyone roared with laughter. Regan assumed Kite's reputation had travelled with him.

Colleen listened. She could hear leaves rustling; she spotted ramblers hiking toward her. She inhaled the sweet aroma and then cautioned herself. The thirst, biting her throat, made them very tempting but there were too many witnesses and too many fatalities only aroused suspicion. Her vampires generally integrated well and it kept any suspicion away from her coven. Their integration ensured she could keep her activities nocturnal, especially with her aversion to sunlight. The rays burned her fragile skin, something other vampires didn't have to worry about since they most had their protection symbols. She had never owned one, having been orphaned a hundred and seventy years before and sent away to live with her sister. As a result she had very few belongings from her human life and certainly no protective amulet.

Colleen kept her position in the shady cover of the tree, still and stealthy. She reassured herself that an animal would suffice that night. But her mouth watered as she imagined savaging one of the ramblers again. She distracted herself and focused on Regan. The thoughts about changing him were reaching her core; her existence controlled by a desire that surpassed her thirst.

He moved in slow motion as he enjoyed a pastime her vampires often participated in. They played with a medicine ball in the forest most nights. The vampires' pace was far superior to humans' and undetectable to their eyes, but she often had to intervene when their games ended in body-crushing fights. They were all very competitive.

Colleen peered down when a dog barked up at her; the noise pierced her ears. She glared and it whimpered but she knew it would not leave. She took flight before anyone noticed her, knowing the dog would not have satisfied her thirst anyway. She whisked through the air like a whirlwind, appearing as a passing cloud of dust to all but two of the footballers.

Colleen varied her hunting grounds to save her from detection. She hunted from the Mourne Mountains, where there were often mountaineers to be lured, to the banks of Lough Erne, which was covered with trees and a perfect hunting ground for her. She could reach one hunting area and venture to another at a speed most humans could not imagine. In fact, she could have been at the other end of

Ireland in no time at all, but that region belonged to the Cavan coven.

She altered her image in keeping with the times; all vamps and vampires did. Sometimes she moved away for a time to prevent her from being recognised. She owned the castle in Glenarm and ruled her coven like a monarch. Beside the castle lay a forest filled with tall dark fir trees which they used as watchtowers over the Glens and the rolling green hills. The sweet scent of the firs mixed with the salty smell of the ocean, together drowned her senses. The pungent aroma of human and animal blood made the village a vamp paradise. Tourists to the area were attracted by the scenery and often fell prey to her and so local losses remained infrequent. She had to dispense with any suspicious humans, however.

Colleen was an experienced huntress. She soared through the trees; her auburn hair blew with the wind; she perched on the branch of a tall fir. She could hear the heart beating, rhythmic and slow. The animal was static, its ears twitched, alerted by her presence. Not human, but it would quench her thirst. Neglecting to feed sapped her energy, but other needs had overwhelmed her thoughts in anticipation of the new arrival. She crouched; ready to pounce. The prey scampered and scrambled through the trees; its ears flapping and its tail bobbing. Then swiftly, she lunged and pinned the deer against the trunk of a tree. A fervent snarl and she sank her fangs into the exposed vein and bled it dry. She'd have to hunt again soon and satisfy her hunger more. She readjusted her silk blouse, feeling slightly more composed. She had a siege to plan so her thirst could wait. Keep or trade? The question buzzed around her head. Male virgins, mature for change, were a rarity and a valuable commodity, although her appetite for young vampires often clouded her judgment.

She darted through the trees. It was a black night without a star. Her night vision assessed the pristine, stony castle as she

landed outside the front door. Friday: Daniel was her
entertainment and her preferred mate. Vamps had little
capacity to love; however, she felt a bond to Daniel, he *almost*
pleased her. She was aware of the Council rule; no special
relationships, and she knew the risk it would pose if she ever
made him aware of her pleasure. Briege had been her
mentor and warned her of the consequences of breaking
Council rules. She was head vamp so Colleen heeded every
word. Briege and Amara, even Amara's brother, although no
one had any idea where he was, were more powerful than
her. Briege stood surety for her with the Vamp Council,
which stood her in good stead and she played a pivotal role
within the Council. Briege had one of largest covens in
Western Europe; Amara had the largest in Africa, having
developed it with Briege's help after she left Belgium. No
one ever knew that the Vamp Council held court in Bruges
under the majestic Bell Tower, though Bruges, or the Dead
City, could not have been more appropriate. The only region
in Western Europe without a coven was Scotland, which they
all avoided.

Kite directed Regan off the coastal road after the ninth glen.
Hunters lay between the Antrim coast and the Causeway
coast. It was somewhat secluded and drew crowds from
surrounding areas.

'It's a straight road once you reach the coast. Just go back
the same way, in case I'm a bit under the weather,' he said.

Five of them had squeezed into Regan's car. 'Just as well
you Irish aren't the biggest in the world,' Regan laughed.

'Dynamite comes in small packages,' Kite snapped. He
and the others were already drinking some liquid concoction
which they hoped would enhance their evening. Regan knew
it would end with him pulling over so one of them could be
sick. He parked the car and they got out; Franky left ahead of
them.

'I'm off to find Fonda. I'll see you later?' Franky called.

'Who's Fonda?' Kite shouted.

'Fonda ... Cox,' he bellowed.

Kite, Regan and the other two boys were bent double.

'He's such a card,' Kite laughed.

Charming Franky was a complete love-rat, the polar opposite of Regan; he made promises but Regan never saw him with the same girl twice. Of course, he was the joker of the group and Kite found his antics hilarious. His crazy sense of humour usually led him astray, often resulting in him getting up to no good. Kite and he were like brothers, although they were complete contrasts. With his long dark hair, dark eyes, and all-year tan Franky didn't look very Irish whereas Kite looked the stereotypical Irishman. Franky used an absurd accent when on the prowl for girls. It was a mixture of German, Spanish and Irish and it baffled Regan how, in such a small country, girls didn't get to know about his awful ways on the grapevine. He must be an amazing lover; Regan could think of no other explanation. He could hear Kite's voice in the background and he turned his attention to him.

'Did you notice how Franky looks part American-Indian,' Kite said.

Kite had hit the nail on the head with his description of Franky.

'Well, the story goes that he was born in America when his father was sent there to work. His mother went along and when his parents moved back from America with him, they told everyone that the American climate had caused him to look like a Native American.' Kite laughed. 'Don't ever say so to Franky; he actually believes it!'

Regan laughed back. Kite was spinning another of his stories. Usually if Kite's mouth moved he was telling some sort of lie.

'He often claims looking like a Native American has a big e

ffect on you. He says it never leaves you without the horn,'
Kite chuckled.

Regan shook his head in disbelief.

'His brain is a little smaller than the rest of ours, I reckon,'
Kite added.

Kite walked away chuckling. They were both, Regan
realised, quite mad.

Nobody really knew the other two boys who were with
them. They did get their names: Ricky and Elvis. They paid
for the petrol so Regan did not complain. Kite did mention
to Elvis that he looked more like a teddy bear than the great
man himself. Unfortunately, everyone spent the rest of the
night calling him Teddy; thankfully he didn't seem to mind.
Ricky, on the other hand, was not amused at being called
Dick the entire night.

They all flirted, danced and tried their best to charm the
ladies, all except Regan; he'd left his heart elsewhere. His
tactic seemed the most effective since the others were getting
nowhere fast; a familiar case of trying too hard. Regan was
pleased when they gave up and decided to go home earlier
than anticipated.

'I could have had anyone I wanted,' Franky whispered to
Kite.

'Aye, the sooner this night's over with the better,' Kite
whispered back.

They nodded in agreement.

Regan drove back the same route. The craic was good, but
he felt exhausted. He dropped the extra passengers at home,
and drove back to Glenarm with Kite and Franky, who were
lying passed out, or so it seemed, on the back seat. The full
moon, which seemed to have appeared from nowhere,
looked painted on the horizon; sitting low and shining
bright. It was eerie as it reflected off the black, motionless sea
which gleamed glass-like without a ripple or a wave breaking
on the rocks. Fog suddenly descended and obstructed his

vision; he turned the lights to bright. He could barely see more than a few yards ahead, so he slowed further. No streetlights and the darkness made the winding road of the coastline more difficult to navigate.

8

The Hunt

Layla considered her recent connection with Regan; the bond she shared with Duncan and Ewan was different; it had no physical bearing. She had a sense of urgency with Regan; thrilling emotion and excitement increased the passion she felt for him. The friend, Franky, worried her and he had to be confronted.

Layla had a dilemma when Regan failed to return. She'd seen Leon serving him in the restaurant but he never probed her about him. It was strange; he *always* interfered in her love life, and she wondered if Regan had been another figment of her imagination. Everything seemed clear one moment, and then in the next it switched to hazy uncertainty. He'd not phoned and she had no way of contacting him. She considered mentioning it to Leon, but reneged on that idea.

Duncan and Ewan were standing on the doorstep.

'Morning, princess,' Duncan said. He smiled a wide, cheerful grin.

'Hi. Come in!'

She was relieved to see familiar faces. They followed her through to the kitchen and she made them a coffee.

'Do you fancy coming to the Highlands with us?' Duncan asked. 'We're going to Ewan's parents for Burns Night. They're having a ceilidh. It should be fun.'

He slurped his coffee.

'When is it?' she asked.

'Stupid question! It's Burns Night. This week … January 25th,' he said.

He lifted a biscuit, dipping and putting it all into his mouth in one go.

Layla shook her head.

'Megan and Sarah are going,' he grumbled, with his mouth full.

'OK. I can't believe it's January. Another year! Where do they go?' she said.

She needed to be with her friends, the ones she was certain were real at that time.

'Holy cow, Layla; you sound like you're a hundred years old,' he said.

She looked at him quizzically.

'How are you?' Ewan asked meaningfully.

His voice was deep and concerned. He changed the subject, seeing her dismay at Duncan's dismissive remark.

'I'm fine,' she lied.

'You look kind of tired.'

Ewan noticed how dark the circles around her eyes seemed.

'I've been working quite a bit, but I'm fine,' she said.

'Want to go to the cinema, Layla?' Duncan said. 'Ewan and I are going!'

She walked over to them and threw her arms around Duncan.

'You're the best friends I could ask for,' she said.

Typical, Ewan thought.

He was always the one concerned and Duncan got the rewards.

Layla was just so grateful that they seemed to know instinctively when she needed company.

Duncan held her tight.

'I know,' he said.

He swung her round, in an attempt to lighten the mood, and she yelped with delight. He was so tall; both he and Ewan were big men and they towered above her like super-humans.

'I'll have to give the cinema a miss though. I promised my aunt I would help her wash her hair,' she said.

The pitch of her voice was high; she was feeling a little guilty. She rubbed her nose persistently.

Duncan laughed.

'You have to be the worst liar in the world, Layla!'

She giggled.

'You know I don't like the cinema. I'll wait for the DVD!'

Ewan laughed too.

They left, telling her that she would have to think of a few rather more persuasive stories for future fibs. She waved them off, thinking of the stories she could, in fact, have told them. They would probably not have believed them anyway.

Ewan pulled up to the front of Layla's early on the 25th. They wanted to get to his parents and make the most of the day ahead. They drove for hours, heading north, further into the Highlands. Cloud and mist lay thicker and heavier in Inverness.

'Did you bring your kilts, girls?' Duncan asked.

'Kilts … never … they would be way too long for us. Layla couldn't wear anything to hide her perfect pins,' Sarah remarked.

Layla slumped frustrated.

'Why are you so shallow?' Megan questioned Sarah.

'OK, Megan, cool down. I meant it as a compliment. She's perfect!'

Sarah's cheeks blushed at Megan's challenge. But the boys were nodding, agreeing with her comments.

'I'm far from perfect. We all bleed the same,' Layla said.

'I'm sorry, I didn't mean to embarrass you,' Sarah said.

Layla's entire face was crimson. 'Haud yer wheesht!' she said.

She turned to Sarah and grinned. The girls snorted and so did Duncan.

'Did you just tell Sarah to shut up?' Ewan said.

'Aye!'

The car began to shake as the subject changed.

'There's another Scot in the back o ... oor ... carrr ... noo,' Duncan chuckled.

When they eventually reached their destination, a few miles east of Inverness, Ewan drove up the stony, winding lane. The estate was like a landscape painting. The residence sat on the crest of a hill with the most magnificent views. It was fit for royalty; Bonnie Prince Charlie could have been standing at the door to greet them. The three girls had not expected anything so grand; the boys had totally downplayed the residence. The estate had been in Ewan's family for hundreds of years, although the house was a little more modern. Duncan's family had been the caretakers for as long as the estate had existed, so Duncan and Ewan were more like brothers than cousins, were both born in the very house they were now looking at.

'Wow!' the girls gasped.

A dishevelled old man opened the aged oak door and ushered them in. They stood awestruck at the entrance of the magnificent hall.

'My whole downstairs could fit in here,' Megan cried out.

A deep burgundy hue warmed the large room. Paintings of the outlying area, encased in antique-gold frames, lined the walls. The staircase began on the polished slate floor and split in the middle, each side leading in opposite directions to the upper level. The banisters were heavy oak and sparkled with polish. The smell of waxy lavender pricked Layla's senses.

The girls smiled at one another as they imagined walking down the staircase in a magnificent ball gown to be met by the hand of a fetching gentleman.

'Ewan, son, how are you?' the hairy old man said. His warm voice almost did not fit with his solemn face. He looked like he'd been pulled through a hedge backwards (indeed tweeting wouldn't have sounded out of place from his nest-like hair).

'Frazer, these are my friends,' Ewan said. He gestured to his friends and they stared at the old man.

'I think you may already be familiar with Duncan!' Ewan chuckled.

'Ach-aye ... that sour face looks very familiar to me,' he said gruffly.

'Aye ... runs in his family,' Ewan laughed. The old man smiled though it didn't come naturally to him.

'Aye ... but fortunately we got the brains, hey Frazer,' Duncan said. 'Our guests, since Ewan forgot about introductions, are: Megan, Layla and the lovely Sarah.'

Sarah smiled a large, open smile.

'Nice to meet you ... all,' Frazer said hesitantly.

'Likewise,' the girls replied.

Layla shuffled on her feet; he made her feel un-comfortable.

'Frazer's the ghillie here on the estate. He's been here since before Duncan or I were born. Part of the furniture, hey, Frazer?'

'Oh, aye, I'm an antique.'

'He's the estate keeper but Duncan and I call him the gatekeeper.'

The ghillie smiled a much easier smile. He studied Layla, unable to take his eyes from her. She felt self-conscious; she rubbed the back of her calf with the toe of her shoe. The girls noticed it but it didn't surprise them. They'd been trying to tell her how often men couldn't take their eyes off her, but she remained unaware. She did not see admiration in the eyes examining her; it felt more like a look of contempt. She sensed his displeasure.

'Where are the family?' Ewan asked.

'Ugh … they went into town to collect the supplies for the caterers. All these doos are that flash noo. The women dinny cook any meer,' the ghillie grumped.

His eyes never faltered from Layla.

'The times they are a-changing, hey, Frazer,' Ewan sang.

'No up here; times dinny change, people do,' he barked.

'History hey … the girls'll have their fill of that tonight,' Duncan said as he tried to lighten the mood.

'Aye!'

Frazer met Layla's gaze; he meant for her to heed every word of the conversation. Duncan detected the animosity.

'Come on, girls … I know where to go … follow me, my bonnie lasses,' he bellowed.

He grabbed Layla's hand, steering her away from the tension. He hurtled up the stairs and pulled her behind him. Her hair brushed her face as he led her to a guest room. They collapsed on a large mahogany bed, dressed in what looked to be the MacGregor sett (the boys called it 'sett' but Layla only knew it as tartan). The room looked spectacular. She felt calmer, protected by Duncan. He and Ewan were like brothers to her.

'Dunc,' she said.

He glared at her.

'Oh right … sorry … Duncan … I forgot!'

'Look if you feel it necessary to call me Dunc I'll not moan anymore. It's obviously a term of endearment. And I know how much you love me.'

He grabbed her, flinging her over the bed for a tickle fight. The other three walked in. Layla and Duncan were in a rather awkward position; the girls laughed loudly. Ewan just stared. The girls jumped on the bed and joined in the fun. Ewan stood apart; reserved.

'So you girls have to share this room,' Duncan said.

He rolled between them.

'Unless one of you would prefer a bit more space, and my room only has one,' he chuckled.

He winked at Sarah.

She blushed; he sniggered at her bashful innocence. Duncan was a predator when it came to girls. His relationships never lasted more than a couple of weeks. He was incapable of commitment.

'I'm sure we'll be fine here. We like doing spoons. Don't we, girls?' Sarah braved.

Megan and Layla giggled at Sarah's courage. Duncan furrowed his brow. The curiosity was getting to him.

'Spoons?' he asked.

'Yeah, spoons … you know when one spoon fits nicely into another and so on,' Sarah said.

She smiled wickedly. Megan and Layla rolled around on the bed; hysterical. Duncan's jaw was hitting the floor. He seemed to be drooling. Ewan's loud, gruff voice laughed at Sarah's impish remark.

'Don't seem so surprised, Duncan. Girls like to cuddle,' Sarah said.

She kept her poker face.

Duncan wiped his mouth.

'Relax, Dunc … she's winding you up,' Layla chuckled.

'You're evil, Sarah Murray,' he smiled.

She returned his warm smile.

'Are there a lot of guests tonight?' Megan said, changing the subject abruptly. There was already enough sexual tension in the group, she thought.

'Not really … just family … but it's always crazy fun,' Ewan said.

After settling in, they took a walk around the estate, with Ewan as tour guide.

'Aye, there's the burn ... at the bottom of the firth, where the glen starts ... you ken?' Ewan said.

He looked at Megan and winked.

Layla was flummoxed.

'What on earth? Could someone please translate?' she asked.

'He's being smart,' Duncan sympathised. 'He's just upping the Scots factor. Some of the families round about still speak Gaelic even, and often at these clan gatherings there's a lot of the language about. But don't worry, most are polite and speak English ... except Frazer; he can't help himself. Anyway, in Lowland Scots he just told you the stream ...'

Layla interrupted. 'Oh, yeah, I forgot *burn* is stream. Oops ...'

'*Firth* is an estuary, and *glen* is a valley. *You ken* is do you understand?' Duncan went on.

'I do now, thanks,' Layla smiled.

She punched Ewan lightly on the shoulder.

'Owww!' he said.

He grabbed his shoulder.

'Oops ... I didn't mean to hurt you. I was just messing around,' she said.

He roared laughing, so she punched him again, harder this time and with a little more intent. It hurt that time, but he held back to save his pride and pretended he didn't feel it. She often surprised him, but he hadn't been expecting her to be so strong.

The estate stunned them with its greenery. It was huge with vast mountains, hills and valleys. A loch, tiny in comparison to Loch Lomond, but just as scenic, lay in front of them. The birds and insects flew around them and grouse ran at their feet.

'Makes you want a whisky. I can feel the warm mist slipping down my throat just thinking about it,' Ewan said.

Duncan told them about the rare golden eagle he'd spotted by the loch a few years previous.

'I was thinking about the venison. There must be plenty of deer here,' Layla said.

They all turned to look at her, bewildered.

'Where'd that come from? I've never met a girl who likes so much protein. We don't really know where you're from. Is it another planet?' Duncan smiled.

'No. My mum's speciality was venison; we ate it a lot,' she explained.

'I'm joking. You don't have to feel bad; we eat loads of venison here,' Duncan said.

'You do?' Megan said. Her face looked horrified. 'I'm a vegetarian!'

'There's a vegetable patch out the back of the kitchen,' Ewan said.

'Oh, thank goodness, I would starve before eating an innocent animal.'

Duncan and Layla laughed.

'I'm a bit surprised by your carnivorous habits, Layla. You do know we have to hunt the venison,' Ewan said.

Duncan laughed again.

'Yeah,' Layla said.

'You'd make a great hunter. We should go … it would be great fun,' Duncan teased.

'Yeah … can we do that?' she said.

She skipped about as Ewan and Duncan looked at one another in disbelief. Then looked back at her, and wondered how they could be surprised; she always acted differently. They'd never managed to convince a girl to hunt with them, ever! Ewan picked up Duncan's vibe as they laughed in amusement.

It would be funny to see what Layla made of the initiation

process, they thought. Would she be as keen when she discovered what it involved?

'If you're up for it; Duncan and I will gladly take you out,' Ewan said.

'I am,' Layla replied quickly; before he changed his mind. 'Let's go then!'

The other girls rejected their offer; they could think of nothing worse than hunting. Ewan assured them they had free run of the house and gave them directions into the village.

'If we leave now we'll get a couple of hours and catch dusk. Dawn or dusk is always the best times for hunting!'

Layla felt a rush of excitement at the thrill of the hunt, plus it would keep her away from the old man for a few extra hours; she trembled at the thought of him.

Layla went to change; the boys instructed her to wear camouflage and not bright clothing. They offered her a kilt and suggested no upper body wear except dirt. She laughed but declined their thoughtful offer, and opted for a tracksuit instead. They told her to meet them in the yard which was out the back of the kitchen. She went downstairs, through the drawing room with its hunt paintings and stag heads on the walls, and into the old farmhouse kitchen. A solid wooden table with twelve chairs filled the middle of the floor. Frazer stepped out from the larder as she entered. She jumped, startled. He stared through her.

'Ewan and Duncan ... um ... asked me to ... um ... meet them in the yard,' she said.

She felt more mouse than man. She couldn't understand his aversion to her, but she sensed it.

'Out back ... are you blind or just stupid?' he said.

She walked toward the back door, quickened her step, then ran out into the yard. Duncan was in the yard, kilted up. Ewan was in the outhouse. Duncan looked at her, bemused.

'What's wrong?'

'That ghillie, he really doesn't like me; he stares at me like

I'm going to eat him.' Duncan put his arm around her shoulders.

'He has a sinister mind. He's dubious of everyone who's not Scottish. Don't take it too personally. The clans and ancestry are all he cares about.'

'Yeah, but it's just me! He seems OK with Sarah and Megan.'

'They're Scottish. OK, so they're Lowlanders but they're still Scots. You're polite with a very unusual accent. He's just assuming you're English and, among others, the English are enemies of Scotland. Some people can't move on.'

She bit her bottom lip.

'But I love Scotland and I'm definitely not English. My accent's a little mixed up but, if anything, my family are Irish, and I thought we were all Celts,' she said.

She frowned.

'Don't be offended, Layla; I know that. Folk who live here, in the Highlands, are a little patriotic. It's all to do with the Stone of Destiny,' Duncan said.

'What's that when it's at home? Maybe you could fill me in later?' Layla asked.

'I could definitely fill you in,' Duncan said. He raised one eyebrow.

'You are a complete pervert,' Layla barked.

Duncan sniggered.

'OK, let's get going, kiddies,' Ewan said as he walked out of the outhouse.

'Hunters – ready,' she bellowed.

'Oh, in the name of great Scots,' Duncan cursed under his breath.

Layla laughed. Ewan joined in and their infectious tee-heeing made Duncan laugh too.

Ewan had a large bucket in his hand. Layla could smell it instantly. He proceeded to paint his body with congealed blood. Layla watched in horror as Duncan followed suit.

'Come on, Layla ... you wanted to come on the hunt,' they said encouragingly.

They stood, gobsmacked, as she lifted the brush, initially with tension on her strained face, and painted some of the blood on. It wasn't so bad; in fact the sweet scent enticed her. She proceeded to cover herself, just as they had. The boys stood, motionless and transfixed. They'd intended to initiate her, to frighten her, lead her to believe they painted themselves every time they hunted. She had just turned the joke on them. Duncan and Ewan laughed hysterically at the sight of her. She stood bemused; she wondered what was so funny. They could not believe how, even covered in crimson goo, she still looked beautiful. Her eyes danced behind the vivid colour that covered her pale face.

'Right, so the second part of the initiation is to take a bite from your first kill.' Duncan would not let her get the better of them. Ewan sniggered in the background. Layla's face was a picture, they certainly had her defeated. They went from the yard into the front garden and past the kitchen window. Layla sensed Frazer watching and turned to see his eyes boring through her. She felt a sudden attack of nausea; he looked at her as if he wanted to do her harm.

Ewan now handed Layla a bow and arrow and a makeshift spear. She furrowed her brow; she stared at her weapons in disbelief.

'Do I look like Robin Hood? What happened to guns?' she said.

'You're more like a bloody-faced rebel,' Duncan said.

'William Wallace?'

The boys laughed, shaking their heads. 'You're crazy, Layla,' Ewan said.

'So they say. Come on, let's dance, boys.' Layla charged with her spear, bow and arrow, shouting with delight. The two boys ran behind her joining in the fun as they headed out into the forest. They were like animated schoolchildren, hooting and roaring with laughter. They only stopped when Ewan suddenly held up his hand for silence.

'OK. Enough, we'll frighten the kill. We'll take turns to shadow you, Layla,' Ewan said.

'No way, I'm great with a compass and I can track too. I don't need a babysitter. I was in the Girl Guides you know,' Layla replied.

'We're only trying to help, Little Miss Stubborn. Here's your compass and a whistle if you need us. We have one too,' Duncan stated.

Her ultra-competitive streak kicked in at that moment.

'May the best hunter win!' she cried.

They noticed the glint in her eye. They didn't dare laugh; she was deadly serious.

'Go forth and conquer the beast,' Duncan jested.

Layla gave him an odd look and walked off as they exchanged glances.

'I'll take the first hour or so,' Ewan said once she had vanished. 'OK, then we can swap over. She probably won't get anything anyway. We've only got a couple of hours before we have to get ready. Turning up like this wouldn't be the best idea, although my Da would appreciate it.' They laughed at the thought of their mothers' faces if Layla walked in covered in blood. 'Hang back, Ewan. If she thinks we don't trust her, she'll be furious.'

'I know, but she'll get lost and we'll spend the night sending out search parties. She's so flaming stubborn,' Ewan complained.

'Independent, I'd say,' Duncan countered. 'That's what makes her special. I've never seen a girl tackle everything like she does. She's got guts. I swear she has no fear.'

'Aye … or perhaps it's just stupidity. She went east so I'll meet you in the middle; if you're not there I'll know you've been successful and give you more time.'

'Aye … you'd better go or you'll lose her,' Duncan quipped.

Ewan shook his head exasperatedly. Duncan had a cheesy grin on his face; Ewan was so easy to wind up. They split up and went in opposite directions.

Layla surveyed the landscape. The hunt required a perceptive and intuitive mind, and she still had no inclination of how powerful those elements within her were. She intended to use all her faculties on this hunt as well as her compass skills. Her eyesight helped as it became sharper even as the light dwindled. She trekked through the foliage with a sense of freedom, feeling elation as the tension within her diminished. She often walked through the parks in Glasgow but that wasn't getting back to nature. Here she felt absolutely free, set loose! She detected a presence; she could hear the resounding heartbeat of an animal. She readied herself to pursue. Suddenly it had disappeared, sensing her approach. She needed to tread more carefully. The heartbeat returned to her ears, and then she heard a second.

Two, she thought.

She approached with caution so not to frighten it off again. Layla crouched among the undergrowth; it came naturally to her. She cast the bow and arrow aside and gripped the spear in her right hand. She listened intently. She could hear each blade of grass move. The deer moved in her direction; she could see it. Its head remained bowed as it fed, unaware of her presence. She waited, telling herself to be patient and stay frozen. When it finally reached her range, she raised the spear, and pounced. A split second and she had it. Her strength surprised her, as she brought the spear up behind her and stabbed its throbbing jugular. Duncan hid behind a tree, watching in disbelief.

She would not taste the warm blood, she thought, although it felt like a magnet to her.

She could hear the other heartbeat louder in her ears; she knew it was human. Her whole life flashed before her.

Suddenly, there was deep realisation, as she finally registered what she was. She remembered the sprite's jugular; she knew what his killer was too! Momentarily she became disoriented but quickly she forced herself to concentrate since Duncan was watching. She would have to keep her discovery for later.

He came from behind the tree and stood in front of her speechless, his jaw hanging open. It was incredible; he'd never seen such an impressive hunt.

'Hi Duncan. I see you couldn't leave me to it, after all. Should I take a bite now?' she smiled.

'If you want to,' he quaked.

'I don't think so but maybe you and Ewan should avoid the tall stories in future,' she smirked.

He looked at Layla, unsure what to make of it all. He didn't really feel in the mood for jokes, but he felt some relief that she didn't want to take a bite.

'Are you sure you've never hunted before?' he said.

'No, why?' she said.

'Could you have been a hunter in a past life?' he said.

'What? What are you on about?' she said.

'Oh ... nothing ... nothing; it's just I've not seen such an impressive hunt. I'm a bit ... I don't know ... surprised; you're a natural,' he said.

She could see his discomfort. She didn't want to make him more suspicious, so she decided to play the dumb blonde card.

'Beginner's luck,' she said, 'or the luck of the Irish. Maybe we should find Ewan; it must be time to get ready.'

'I have my whistle; I'll call him,' he said.

He blew hard on the whistle and it echoed through the valley; Ewan would detect it. He'd lost his sense of humour; for once he'd let the opportunity to exploit a double entendre – talk of blowing his whistle – go by. She knew he was unnerved by what he had witnessed.

'I feel really dirty now. Do you take the carcass back with you?' she said.

'Aye,' he answered.

Duncan went over to examine the deer. The blood drained from his face when he saw the wound. It was an effective way to kill the animal, but how? He tried to reassure himself that it was inexperience, but his mind didn't want to process it. He looked at her doubtfully; she seemed like an accomplished hunter. Layla had never lied to him since they'd met; surely she couldn't be lying now. He removed the spear from its neck while her back was turned and stuck his arrow into the deer's ribcage. He knew Ewan would ask too many questions if he saw how Layla capably killed the animal with a single blow to the jugular vein, and he had no answers for him. He would probe Layla when they got back to Glasgow. He decided to put the conclusions he'd jumped to at the back of his mind; it was not the time to deal with his thoughts. Burns Night was too significant for their families.

Ewan was approaching.

'Hi!' Ewan shouted.

His deep voice echoed around the trees and he waved energetically.

'Did you get anything?'

Layla smiled. 'Did you?' she called back.

'Naw ... I wasn't fast enough,' he said.

He laughed heartily as he ran toward them.

Duncan tried to regain a sense of equilibrium, telling himself to get it together. By the time Ewan came over he'd managed to hide his concern.

'By the way I never even asked: did you, Duncan?' she said.

'Na, I was instructed to tail you, but there was obviously no need,' he said.

'Wow, well done, Layla. That's what I get for mocking you.'

'So I win then,' she said.

'Aye ... you win,' Ewan said.

She was doing a tribal dance round the carcass. Ewan was laughing. Duncan found it strange. Ewan and Layla carried the carcass. She carried it with ease and would have managed it to the house without a wince, but she had to keep her cover to throw Duncan off her scent. After a few hundred metres Layla dropped the hind legs, puffing and panting.

'I can't, I'm done,' she said.

Duncan picked up the rear as she pretended to collapse to the ground with exhaustion. They dropped the deer and waited for her.

'Just give me a minute, I think it's just hit me; I'm going to …'

She ran, bent over and imitated retching. She walked back as she wiped her mouth on her sleeve.

'Are you all right?' Duncan said.

Ewan handed her a tissue.

'Yeah … I just … I can't believe …' and then waterworks.

At that moment she remembered her previous tears, bloody tears. She held her tissue tightly against her eyes just in case. She couldn't let them see. Duncan put an arm around her. She felt relieved after seeing the devastation in his face. She pushed the tissue to her face, tighter.

'I'll be fine. I just need to clean up. Let's go back now,' she said.

She was glad there was already blood on her face; they would not have noticed any extra splats.

'You walk in front, that way you won't see it,' Duncan suggested.

Ewan agreed.

9

Once Bitten

Colleen was lurking on a hill along the coast road. She positioned herself among the trees, waiting on the last bend approaching Glenarm. She could see the road winding in front of her, and she waited patiently. She saw the red car; distant to the naked eye, but perfect in her night vision. She heard him humming as he tapped the steering wheel; his heartbeat almost in unison with the tapping. In a flash, she swung round and kicked a tree with brutal force. Bang! It fell over and then another and another. The two idiots were not meant to be in the car and she was angry. She had to contain herself. She could see the car slowing down again; just as well or her hunters would have had a serious problem. The fog was beneficial to her, since it would render her practically invisible to any witness.

She readied herself as the car approached. She scanned the area again; she dare not risk any interruption. The impact to the car needed to be perfect; she would not jeopardise his life. A fatality would be disastrous. A beating heart was the only way to initiate the change, and she'd never had a virgin. Her powerful hand pulled the car to a halt.

Ah, just right, she thought.

He banged the steering wheel, furious. What now?

He looked back at his friends; they didn't as much as blink.

Drunken sods! He got out to check for damage. All thought ceased as he stared in disbelief: a figure loomed before him. He was frozen with shock as it grabbed his throat; then … blackout!

She ascended the hill; laid him by a tree and flew back through the air. She hissed as she threw a couple of punches at the two losers sitting in the back, and they, suddenly waking from their stupor, took flight. She threw the car into the sea and smashed a hole in the wall along the sea edge, leaving evidence of an impact. A police and coastguard search would be underway by morning; she'd seen it before. When they dredged the nearby coastline they would find the car; a mere formality. The Irish Sea had claimed a number of victims in her existence; the currents were terribly dangerous.

As she ascended the hill, she persuaded herself to go slower.

'Rare and valuable … rare and valuable', she chimed over and over to quieten her frenzy.

She would bleed with caution; it enhanced subservience. Her rules were harsh and non-negotiable; despicable punishment was the consequence of defiance. He would never be allowed to indulge in human blood: abstinence diluted aggression and ensured her continued dominance.

He lay moaning beneath the towering fir tree. The dark blinded him, but he felt a presence in his semi-conscious state. She approached him and gradually placed her slender, pallid hand over his mouth to silence him. She masked the horror with her seductive performance as irresistible femme fatale.

Regan felt aroused; it seemed erotic. He sensed danger but this only intensified his stimulation. Was she a woman? he thought; she had the face of a beautiful woman. His discomfort pleasured her. She placed her icy frame on his. As she sat astride him, he could feel her athletic form stimulating his loins. It reminded him of someone, her form seemed familiar. She ran her cold tongue along his face. His heart beat like a racehorse.

She was an auburn beauty, an Irish colleen, but her eyes were dark and alarming. For all her 'good' intentions she could not disguise the wild passions within her and her true foul being broke through her fair countenance. She felt her throat burn as it craved to take his blood, and unguarded now she flashed her shiny, white weapons. His pupils dilated in terror as he saw his fate. Horror engulfed him as in one, smooth, rapid movement she pushed his head up to reveal the vein pumping in his neckline and sank her venomous fangs into it. No pain at first, but when the ferocious venom entered him the agony was immeasurable. His writhing struggle below her thrilled her as she drained the mortal life from him, slowly and steadily. The venom spread and paralysed him. His blood-curdling screams echoed through the forest and all wildlife scampered, so she put her hand over his mouth. A demonic sadist, she revelled in every agonising moment, savouring each mouthful of blood, knowing that eventually she had to stop. The black bile consumed him. It would not be long, she thought. He went limp and she withdrew. The bleed had been even more effective than she had anticipated; her patience had been remarkable and she congratulated herself.

She had to get him back to the castle before the transition began. His cries would be more deafening and audible to human ears. She lifted him aloft and swiftly flew through the trees. She studied his liquid appearance, realising how breathtaking he was going to be. His new form would solidify as the change established itself and his features would become defined and flawless.

Sheer perfection, she thought. He was unique and she wouldn't mind waiting for him. None of the other covens in the British Isles, or indeed the whole of Western Europe, had a virgin vampire. The envy of her fellow vamps would result in a ferocious bidding war. She already knew she would not give him up – to anyone, for any price.

10

Burns Night

Layla soaked in a warm bubble bath. She excused herself, having told the boys her head was spinning, but, if anything, it cleared up her feelings of folly. Something felt different, as if she had made a discovery, although she could have imagined a better time and place for the revelation. She finally understood what she was and how she felt, and she knew who it was that would have some explanation for her.

Layla didn't sit easy with attending the gathering. She didn't know if she had enough stability at the moment to socialise with strangers. She knew Megan and Sarah would harass her until she changed her mind, so she got dressed anyway. She felt somewhat indecisive, but that was nothing new.

'Oh good, you're ready,' Sarah said as she and Megan entered the room.

'Are you OK?'

Layla nodded.

'The hunt was a bad idea,' Layla answered, exiling for the moment the feeling of exhilaration the hunt had given her.

'I don't know how you did it,' said Sarah with a shudder.

She didn't answer as she watched Megan packing up her bits and pieces.

'Are you going somewhere, Megan?' Layla asked.

'Ewan's two cousins can't make it so we each get a room of our own,' Megan whooped.

Layla felt relief. She had begun to wonder how she would have managed to lie beside them with their scents invading her senses.

'Shall we go?' Layla asked.

'I'm starving. I could eat a scabby horse,' Sarah giggled.

'Ugh ... I'll be sick,' Megan yapped. 'Sa ... rah ... you know how I feel about animals. I don't know how you're going to eat after what you just did, Layla,' Megan said.

She glared at Layla as though she'd carried out an execution. Megan couldn't agree with killing animals; it was as well she had no idea of Layla's real thoughts on the subject.

'My stomach's bigger than my eyes,' Layla replied.

'I don't know about that. Sometimes your eyes shine so much that they almost cover your face. Mine are like slits.'

Sarah prised her eyes open with two fingers.

'You have lovely eyes, Sarah,' Layla insisted.

'Enough about eyes. As I recall, you both gave me a hard time earlier about commenting on appearance. What was it you said? Aye ... you're so shallow!' Sarah said.

'Point taken,' Layla said.

'Come on, let's go to this party.'

Megan was getting impatient.

Ewan and Duncan were standing in the corner of the room, looking very dapper in their family setts. They wolf-whistled softly as the girls approached them. The girls giggled. They'd each bought new LBDs for the black-tie affair. Layla recognised the boy's kilts from other functions where there was always an array of different tartans but she noticed that there were only two tartans in the room that night. Ewan introduced them to his hospitable family. The girls were baffled by his uncle, unsure if he was speaking to them in Gaelic or just whisky-tongue. Duncan introduced his parents, who were just as friendly.

The maître d' tapped a crystal glass to invite them into the dining room. Layla winced, as the sound rang in her ears. They walked through the large reception room, warmed by a huge roaring fire. The walls were covered with hessian with white cornicing and were dressed with the stately portraits of old family members.

A piper skirled the bagpipes and piped each couple into the dining room. Ewan, being the perfect gentleman, placed Layla's arm through his and led her through to the dining room. Duncan took Sarah's arm in a similar fashion and he'd arranged for his cousin Robert to escort Megan. The dining room was dressed for royalty as Ewan ushered Layla to her seat. He stood by her side and waited while the other ladies were escorted in. As she sat at the huge mahogany table, Layla scanned the room. It was decorated with candelabras and floral arrangements of white rosebuds and thistles. She soaked up the ambience, admiring the large chandeliers which softly lit the room. The glassware and silver cutlery gleamed, polished to perfection, as the light reflected from them. Layla looked up at the chandeliers; she could see every microscopic detail and turned her gaze away when she felt the light piercing her pupils. She could smell pungent scents of smoke and the sweet aroma of heather and metallic salt; this unnerved her.

Her attention was distracted when she recognised the piper: it was the old ghillie; she'd not recognised him at first. She shifted restlessly in her chair; he was wearing the MacGregor sett. Duncan hadn't mentioned him as a relation. She dipped her head, trying to escape his suspicious menacing stare and hoped he would be sitting away from her. She sat at one end of the table, with Ewan's family, while Megan and Sarah sat at the other, with Duncan's. She wished they had all been together, for moral support, but his presence changed her mind. She was glad there would be distance between them; he would certainly be sitting with Duncan's family.

She diverted her gaze and noticed the makeshift dance floor, remembering she had no idea how to dance Scottish reels and jigs.

Finally, when all the guests were seated, Ewan's father made a welcoming speech and the first course was served. Layla no longer felt hungry, but she spooned the Scotch broth into her mouth to be polite. She smiled to Megan and Sarah and ignored the soup catching in the back of her throat. Ewan was attentive; he told her to leave what she couldn't eat, assuming she was still sickened by the hunting expedition. Layla looked at him with appreciation.

'You look breathtaking, Layla. Your eyes are so dark, they match your dress.'

'Thank you, Ewan. You look handsome yourself. I can see where you get your good looks. You're very like your mother; you have her brown eyes and dark hair. There is a possibility yours is longer than hers though,' she giggled.

He chuckled in his thick tones.

'There's no punishment for laughing, Layla,' he assured her.

'Mum,' he bellowed, over the chatter and goings on in the room.

'Layla says my hair's nicer than yours,' he laughed.

Layla shot him daggers. She was enraged. The ghillie's severe eyes lingered on her.

'I said no such thing, Mrs MacGregor,' she said.

She fiddled with her emerald necklace and regained her composure. His mother gave her a broad smile.

'Don't worry, dear. I've told him to get that hair fixed on countless occasions.'

Layla smiled, focusing on her gentle voice. 'Sorry, Layla,' Ewan whispered, 'I couldn't resist. You seem a little jumpy. Is Frazer still glaring at you?'

'How did you know?'

'Duncan mentioned it to me earlier, but a blind man would see it. Then again, I'm not surprised he can't take his eyes of you in that dress. It should be illegal to wear that. Have you not noticed that most of the men have been looking at you tonight?'

She shuffled in her chair again.

'Ewan, would you give it a rest? We all look good enough to eat; you're embarrassing me,' she stated and then added a gentle giggle when she saw the bemused look on his face.

'OK, keep your hair on,' he chuckled.

His laugh was soft; he did not want to embarrass her further.

'I think you're the one with problems in that department,' she smiled.

Layla looked at Duncan and he glimpsed at her. She smiled but he turned away. He seemed subdued and he was usually the life and soul. She hoped he'd been forewarned by his family to behave and she relaxed a little, the ghillie's view of her had been blocked by other diners.

The second course, and she definitely felt like she'd relaxed too soon. The ghillie was on his feet again, proudly piping in the haggis. It was brought to the table and placed in front of Ewan's father, the host of the evening. He had the honour of reciting Robbie Burns' famous poem and acted out his part with vigour and a dagger. They toasted one another with whisky and the haggis was served. Layla would have preferred it rare but she tasted it all the same. The whisky however was quite 'more-ish' and she drank it as Ewan refilled her glass. It seemed to settle her nerves somewhat. Megan kept to the neeps and tatties; her face showed her stomach was very uncomfortable with the fact that it was a stuffed sheep's belly. Duncan's cousin delighted in teasing her and the colour drained from her face still further.

The main course of venison could not have been any worse for Megan. She had to excuse herself and she ran to the ladies'. Mr MacGregor tapped his glass to make an announcement.

116

'I realise I have already welcomed you all so this is a short announcement. This evening's venison has been supplied after a successful hunt by our very own ghillie. I'm sure you'll all join me in a round of applause for Frazer.'

The guests applauded.

'I'd also like to take this opportunity make a toast to the lassies and in particular Ewan's friend, Layla, our newest hunting recruit to these hills. Ewan assures me she will be quite useful for future venison supplies. Please stand, my dear, so we can raise a toast to you and the other lassies in our company tonight.'

Layla's legs turned to jelly.

'Stand up, Layla; don't be shy!' Ewan said encouragingly.

He was tapping her arm. She glared at him. He stood up and placed his hand in hers, helping her to her feet. He whispered gently that she would be fine. Layla got to her feet for Ewan's sake; she did feel better with him standing beside her. He knew how Layla never felt comfortable being the centre of attention, although her appearance made that difficult. Ewan's father raised his glass and toasted Layla. He clearly found it hard to believe that such a striking young girl could be such an accomplished huntress.

'Duncan informs us that you are a very capable hunter,' Mr MacGregor added.

She gave a graceful, appreciative nod, keeping her eyes from the ghillie's, and was just about to return to her seat when Ewan whispered that tradition dictated the lassies raise a toast to the laddies.

Duncan felt for Layla. He'd been dubious about her hunting skills, but he knew she would be feeling very uncomfortable. He tried to help her compose herself by giving her a warm smile. She returned the gesture and sighed.

'Thank you Mr MacGregor for your kind words, the other lassies and I would like to raise a toast to you and the other esteemed gentlemen in the room, excluding Ewan of course ...'

Mr MacGregor guffawed as the other guests laughed aloud, except the ghillie, then he never seemed amused about much.

Ewan clapped loudly and shouted, 'To all the lassies!'

Layla raised her glass, 'To all the laddies,' and giggled as all the guests raised their glasses and chimed a reply adding in lassie or laddie depending on their gender.

The ceilidh started. Layla insisted that Ewan dance with Megan; she had no idea how to dance the reels. She tried a couple of dances with Robert, but Frazer's eagle eyes didn't help.

More ringing in her ears as the glass was tapped again.

'Excuse me, ladies and gentleman.' He began to speak in Gaelic and Ewan came over to the girls to translate. 'Gentlemen, being a traditionalist, I invite you to join me in the smoking room for a whisky and a cigar.'

All the men filed out leaving the women to dance alone. Megan and Sarah partied with their shoes off.

Layla needed to find a bathroom; she felt a little ruffled and needed to make up her face a little. She giggled to herself as she tried to find her way around the house, wandering from room to room. It would have been easier to find her way outdoors. She gave up and decided to use the bathroom in her room. She ran upstairs and opened the door, then suddenly realised she'd turned right, instead of left, on the landing. Thankfully she'd walked into a large bathroom. She fixed her hair and her panda eyes (without much success) and then washed her hands. She looked for a towel but had to wipe her hands on her dress.

Muffled voices sounded in her ears and she tried popping them. She realised it was coming from the next room. Her ears pricked up as the voices raised and the conversation became more heated; men debating. She couldn't help but listen. They were talking about a code or in code, a Highland Code. There was a lot of Gaelic which she couldn't understand. They switched back and forth between Gaelic and English. They discussed developments in the area and various other matters.

As she opened the door to leave, they began to disperse. She gently pushed the door, holding the handle down, to evade their view, not wanting to show she had been ear-wigging. So she waited for silence but as she held the door ajar, she heard another voice, a familiar gruff voice, and noted that not everyone had left the chamber. Her stomach somersaulted; her blood turned to ice as a more ominous topic of conversation commenced. It was the ghillie.

'Vampires!' he cried out with scorn. 'There seems to be evidence they live among us. Our tumultuous relations with these creatures in the past led to an encounter which was supposed to deter their return. I am of the opinion that we should deal with them now to avoid a final catastrophe. We should not have to summon our ancestors; that is the point of our existence. We need to agree on a course of action!'

Layla gasped; she put her hand over her mouth. Then she heard Duncan's voice, clear as crystal, in her ears.

'They've brought us nor Scottish people any harm. Why destroy them when they hide their existence to avoid conflict with us. We know only too well about suffering of our people in their own country when England tried to destroy Scotland. If their intention was to cause our people any harm they would have become active long before now!'

Layla listened intently. What she had seen in the city centre contradicted Duncan but it confirmed for her that Franky was just as she had perceived. Her head was spinning; she heard a third voice and had no idea how she stayed upright.

'We don't need the trouble. One of ours created the vamps instead of destroying them, gave them freedom and power, and now we can't take risks. We've obviously not been a strong enough deterrent for them. If we do not eradicate the vampires, a vamp may take her chances here. We are supposed to be Protectors and I say we protect!'

She did not know Ewan could speak such callous words. She'd been blind to his brutality. The capacity of her mind broadened as she realised she may be that vamp.

'We should discuss this sooner rather than later to finalise our decision. There was an incident in Glasgow. It all sounds a little familiar to me but there is no evidence to confirm it. We should hold the next meeting at the Stone of Destiny in keeping with concealment. Our fellow Scotsmen don't know of the power bestowed upon us, they do not know Highlanders exist or vamps and vampires for that matter. They have no idea that Burns Night may be the night Robbie Burns was born but was also the night Myntie MacIntosh was burned to extinction by our kind. The 25th of January is a significant date for the Highlanders because we destroyed the vampire and exorcised his control. I think it best to keep it that way. If we don't destroy these beings again many of our people could come to great harm. We have to find the right time to execute them.'

The voice was the ghillie's. She believed he'd seen what she was from the outset but she could not fathom why he had not revealed her true nature to them.

'Aye ... I agree,' Ewan confirmed.

His voice was formal and Layla shuddered.

'I need some time,' Duncan's voice vibrated; he seemed troubled.

Layla flew into the guestroom before they could vacate the chamber. She wanted to go back to Glasgow. She hoped she would awake to find it had all been a nightmare. She locked the door, climbed into bed and tried to hide. She tossed and turned, afraid of what lay in her wake. She could not leave until morning or it would only have aroused suspicion. She could hear the cheer, and smell the gathering, the putrid stench of smouldering hatred hidden in the Highlanders and that deterred her further. The recitations of Burns' poetry seemed irrelevant and she was glad to hear the closing speech, which was followed by silence.

She pored through the events since she arrived. The ghillie ... the hunt ... the look of horror on Duncan's face ... the Highlanders and the return of the ancestors and realised that Duncan and Ewan had kept her in the dark too. She felt woozy as she writhed, twisting and thrashing again. She wondered if it was the final stage of her losing her mind as her body lay drenched in a cold sweat and her heart repeatedly palpitated then slowed to a silent drum.

First light appeared and she placed a note on the dressing table. Her instincts emerged as she crouched in the open window and left. She leapt, spiralling through the air and landed on her feet, poised for the next movement. Her reflexes were automatic and she darted through the estate, fleeing to the cover of the Lowlands and the city.

11

Transformation

Colleen arrived back at the mansion where Jimmy, Colin and Daniel had prepared a room. The change was underway: all the colour had drained from his face as his complexion became more pallid and his lips darkened. Within a day his fine and masculine features had cleared, almost to perfection. The other vampires checked him regularly, seeing his agony and knowing how excruciating it was. Colleen was just focused on the end result.

A million swords slashed his insides and flesh-eating beetles feasted on his brain, for what felt like endless torture. He lay paralysed and slowly the suffering dulled to an ache. He trans-vampired within a few days; they had never witnessed such a rapid change.

His eyes opened and his vision pierced through every item in the room. He could've heard a pin drop miles away. His frame hardened to resemble concrete.

Daniel entered the room; Regan snarled and growled as his mind raced.

Where was the beast? *What* was it? It didn't sound like a lion or even a bear; it sounded like nothing he'd heard before. He felt the rattle in the back of his throat just as his body went off on its own tangent, thrashing and convulsing. His thoughts became distorted as he visualised the attractive woman and remembered the seduction. He shuffled uncomfortably, remembering the pleasure. Then, the perfect white teeth, the long incisors, and his mind raced again. He remembered it all: the girl and the horror. He looked around, his eyes darted back and forth, as he imagined that it all must be a nightmare. What the hell? It must be hell, he thought.

Jimmy his brother stood before him.

Oh no, I *am* dead!

He studied the ghostly form. It was definitely Jimmy. Images of strangers and places flashed before him. He felt a needle pierce his lip and his body thrashed. One final thrash and he broke free.

As he crouched, the others mirrored him and he softened his pose. There were three of them in the room. He studied them intently and his thoughts posed questions and answered them at the same time.

Perfect, colourless humans … but not humans! he thought.

They had numerous similarities but were not identical. He glanced at Jimmy again. He wondered if his mother's human eyes would recognise her son but he knew they would not, especially in a drunken stupor. Regan considered the irony of the situation. It was as if a clothed Michelangelo's David stood before him; Jimmy had used to spend all his spare time in the gym trying to perfect his physique; now he was perfect, unblemished. He smiled at Jimmy, feeling a strange sense of pride and delight.

Regan knew it could not be a nightmare, he thought he'd lost his brother for ever and yet he had just been hidden from him. They recognised their mutual delight at seeing one another again. Regan could tell by his brother's boyish smile.

Jimmy flashed him a warning glance, his code when they were children for Regan to keep a secret. Regan raised his right thumb to his mouth and touched his bottom lip, the same way he always did when confirming he'd received Jimmy's signal. Jimmy knew that, if Colleen realised they were brothers, it could be fatal for both of them.

Colleen sailed into the room. 'He seems really calm even with such a rapid transformation. I expected him to be more volatile. It seems I don't know everything after all!' Colleen said with a laugh. She was often amused by her own statements.

The other vampires remained silent, waiting for Daniel's prompt. Only when he laughed, did they laugh, though it rang hollow.

'Colleen, you always know everything; I've never known you to get anything wrong.'

Regan quickly sussed that Daniel was a bit of brown nose and he crinkled his brow. Who was she anyway, other than a control freak?

He felt irritable as he heard the rattle in the back of his throat again.

'Maybe we could release him. He seems safe enough,' she said.

Daniel went to unlock the cuffs, but soon realised that Regan had already broken free of them. He disclosed nothing, however. Catching on, Regan rubbed his wrists extravagantly. They all watched, each trying to anticipate his next move.

'I'll be in the other room,' Colleen said. 'Bring him to me when he's ready. You know your instructions.'

In one fluid movement, at speed, he leapt to his feet; his astonishment at its strength visible in his marvellous smile. Maybe this wasn't so bad, he thought.

The others observed him dubiously; unsure of how trustworthy he was.

'If we hadn't watched him change I would query his vampirism,' Daniel said.

Regan was stretching his limbs, feeling his new strength and suppleness.

'This is bizarre. I feel like I could run through a concrete wall,' he yelled.

The other vampires blocked their ears.

'Turn the volume down a little. You have to control everything by clarifying it in your mind. All your senses have increased to new levels,' one of the other vampires suggested in a sing-song Kerry accent.

His name was Padar, and he was Colleen's longest serving vampire, her first to add to her coven. He'd been gifted to her by her mentor and sister, Briege.

They laughed; they all warmed to him immediately.

'My voice! ... where's my accent?' He lowered the volume and his voice wavered a little. His accent was an odd mixture but the words seemed to just roll off his tongue.

'It's your vocal cords; they've altered with the rest of you. It's like being from another country or another world really,' Jimmy explained.

Regan's jaw dropped when he heard his brother speak; he sounded different too. Jimmy gave him a look; Regan closed his mouth.

Regan's throat grated; he'd never felt so thirsty before.

'I am so thirsty,' he said. He held his hands around his throat. 'I have the strangest sensation in my throat!' All he knew was that he needed to relieve the pain.

The other vampires chuckled but Jimmy looked at Regan solemnly.

Daniel explained that the pain was his thirst for blood.

Oddly Regan did not feel troubled; he just wished they would show him how he could stop the agonising, burning thirst.

Daniel produced a live rat. Regan could smell it. It didn't appeal to him but he could hear its heart. Instantly, he sunk his jagged fangs into its vein and drank vigorously. He looked at the vampires in earnest and Jimmy left. He'd no sooner gone than he returned with three hares. He could hear they had more liquid rushing through their veins.

'Mmmm … yum … Isn't there something a little more … appealing?' he moaned.

He executed them regardless and their blood soon dripped from his chin.

The others knew that his relief would be short-lived. He needed to indulge his natural hunting instincts – they would take him into the forest.

'Your thirst is harder to satisfy initially,' Daniel said, 'and your hunting instincts will be heightened until you've given chase for the first time. Both will ease over time. Transformation usually means you need to satisfy your thirst more frequently, but that will ease too. But humans are forbidden, Regan. That is a fundamental rule and it cannot, under any circumstances, be broken. You will have to be tested before you can encounter humans again.'

Regan looked mystified, but not concerned; he couldn't imagine drinking *human* blood at all. Jimmy knew that the smell of mortal blood had not yet pierced his nasal passages but that once it had he would become the polar opposite of the rational vampire he seemed to be at that moment.

'He's very calm,' Padar said, 'but that might change, I wouldn't take any chances of allowing him to be with Colleen for a while. We should probably wait a while.'

They all wondered how Regan would react when he discovered his true fate. That his existence would, ultimately, be one of submission; just like theirs. All but Daniel had at one point or another wished for death, but they had never been given the opportunity. Colleen never allowed her mates to make any decisions; only she could decide when a vampire's time had expired.

Any rebellion, Jimmy knew, would bring a terrifying fate.

Colleen would not hesitate to approach the Council to ask for the punishment of any mate who had overstepped the mark. The Council would be only too happy to have the opportunity to demonstrate their control; executions served to deter any potential rebels by branding images of the torture on their minds; they ensured vampires were firm about the rules with one another.

Jimmy knew the other vampires were perceptive and would soon work out the link between them. He knew too that Regan would rue his existence as much as he did. Colleen's control included what they were able to consume and so she was able to dilute their natural aggression and strength as well as quell their desires and minds.

To Colleen, Daniel appeared her only true loyal servant and she used him to keep the others in line. In truth, his motivations were more complex and he feared that eventually Regan would replace him.

On the vampires' instructions, in the presence of Colleen Regan always kept up the façade of the 'untamed' vampire, still in the early stages of his transformation. Colleen suspected no foul play, especially as many transitions took time. A few days after Regan's arrival she summoned Daniel to her chamber.

'Daniel, I've been called to a meeting with the Council. I won't be long,' she said.

'Are you going by conventional means or your own?' he asked.

'My own. I'm meeting Briege in Dublin harbour at midnight. We might call in at the Moulin Rouge on our way back,' she snorted. 'After all I am a true lady of the night.'

Daniel laughed.

'Regan must be getting more subdued. Perhaps I should see him before I leave?' she said.

She had reservations about leaving her coven with an

immature vampire, especially since she had no connection to him as she did with the rest of the coven.

Daniel's face was fixed; he concealed his thoughts and Regan's abilities. If she knew he was capable of hiding anything from her she would have found it intolerable. His resolute mind as a human had followed him into his vampire existence and he only allowed her to be more powerful than him purely because of his devotion to her. He was too jealous to share her with another mate and he knew Regan's value; he did not want to lose her favour.

'He's not ready. It's still too risky for you,' he said.

'He's very valuable, Daniel. You do understand, don't you? I could get one of Briege's vamps to come up.'

Daniel knew that would have been a bad idea; they were even more vindictive than Colleen. The last execution carried out by Briege's vamps had been brutal.

'What if she abused your coven? Regan is still vulnerable. Was there not a coup within our kind before?'

'Yes, once; you have a point,' she agreed.

'Have I let you down before?' Daniel persisted.

He flashed a seductive smile, which easily distracted her from the truth. He knew that she could not escape her own desire. Colleen was never sure, but Daniel did something to her, something she did not recognise. He was why she sought more such similar mates and yet he himself had not been a virgin.

12

Realisation

Her aunt sat in the living room and she saw a shadow cast over the window … and then vanish. A fraction of a second later Layla was standing before her.

'Layla, what's wrong? What happened?'

'I think you might want to get a doctor now.'

'You're probably tired. Ceilidhs *are* tiring.'

'No I'm definitely not tired; I've never had more energy. It's these strange things I'm seeing; now it's Highlanders. One minute I know who I am; the next I don't.'

Layla rubbed her palms together over and over and over again. Aunt Kate stood up, ushered her to a chair and gently prompted her to sit down. She didn't need to sit and she pulled away. Kate put her hands over the top of Layla's to stop the constant motion; she patted her hands. She persisted and motioned Layla to sit; Kate sat facing her. Layla's ears were ringing and just as suddenly they pricked up. She heard voices in the distance. Again she rubbed her hands and pinched her skin forcefully, but it did not create silence. She looked out the window and saw two young girls at the end of the road. She could hear every word they said.

'It's true,' Layla whispered.

Aunt Kate sat silent and motionless.

'What?' Layla bellowed.

She sprang from the chair but Kate, still in silence, forced her to sit down again.

'Calm down, Layla,' she murmured. She raised her voice slightly. 'Layla … clear your mind. You're flitting from one thought to another; you have to simplify your thoughts.'

Layla took slow, deep breaths, steering herself away from the panic she could feel in her chest. Her mind raced; her breathing rapid, she could hear her heart pulsating, she perspired and her mind spun like a cog in a wheel. Before Kate could even register her movement, she'd risen and disappeared.

'Layla!' she shouted.

She knew Layla would hear her.

'Come back now! You're being irrational!' She'd barely finished the sentence and Layla stood in front of her.

'I know … that's my point,' Layla bellowed.

'Shush,' Kate said. Her aunt had her finger over her mouth. 'You'll alarm the neighbours.'

'I'm alarming myself.'

She flew from one end of the room to the other in a flash.

'Layla, you can slow it down. Look, I'm proof,' she said.

'What?'

'You've been slowing yourself naturally without evening realising. You're just over-thinking it all now, where before you slowed everything down.'

Kate took off and almost instantly reappeared beside her. Layla's eyes sparkled in astonishment.

'Being patient is a learned behaviour and it's essential to exist in this society,' Kate said.

'Why didn't you tell me? I have been in turmoil,' she said.

A light grumbling growl was rising in the back of Layla's throat; she snarled. Immediately she put her hand over her mouth.

'I was worried about you going to the Highlands. I knew it would be upsetting for you.'

'You mean you know about *them* too?' Layla roared.

'Layla … calm down. I assure you I am stronger than you,' she warned.

Layla stood firm. He aunt did not move, giving her the opportunity to stand down. It took a while.

'Now close your eyes and relax. Try to hypnotise yourself. Relax through it. Your mind is vast. Beyond comparison to your human mind and I had to let you make your own discovery. You've been changing for a while. I've not seen another change like yours, although all changes are unique; but yours seems to indicate it started at birth, as opposed to death.'

Layla gasped with exasperation. She found it all so unbelievable but at the same time she now had the ability to process the information. The only way she could ever truly make sense of anything was to be on her own. With a swift reproachful glance at her aunt she ran to her room.

Night fell but sleep eluded her. She had no need for rest. She had a dire need, an insatiable desire for blood. She could smell the sweet aroma of a young girl walking past the window. Her eyes observed every inch of her. Her ears could hear the boom … da … boom of her heart and her tongue could taste the warm, salty metal juice pulsing through her veins.

Her aunt appeared in front of her. Layla was crouching, she did not alter her stance; she snarled, wanting to pounce, but when something sharp nicked her bottom lip, she startled. She was suddenly standing, upright, shoulders back and head held high. Her aunt held her position for a time.

'Don't even think about it!'

Layla looked at her in surprise.

'I'm OK … I slowed it down … I'm fine!'

Her tone had levelled off a little.

'Impressive … I thought you may have needed to fight your emotions more,' her aunt said.

The surprise was written over Kate's face.

'My mouth is so dry. I'm so thirsty!'

Layla rubbed her fingers over her throat. Her aunt disappeared and as Layla turned round she was standing in front of her with a large glass of orange juice. Layla downed it, in one gulp.

'No. No good!' Layla's head was shaking fiercely.

'I know it won't take the thirst away, but it will help you steer clear of mortal blood,' her aunt explained.

When Layla asked how, her head tipped sideways. Her aunt placed the palms of her hands on each of Layla's cheeks and straightened her head back. Layla snarled.

'Hey ... cheeky!' Aunt Kate said.

Layla giggled. 'Oh ... sorry,' she said.

Layla's disappointment showed on her solemn face.

'It's the vitamin C in the orange juice. It helps the animal blood to give you some strength not just sustain you. Mortal blood is ...'

Layla was confused but she would take her word for it.

'Come with me, Layla.'

She dashed out the door and Layla followed as they flew through the quiet backstreets. They ran, invisible to the human eye, dust whirling behind them. Kate led her to the nature reserve at Loch Lomond.

When they arrived at the loch Layla's natural instincts took over. She suspended herself in a branch of a tree overhanging the loch.

'We must remain in the nature reserve, Layla. We cannot cross the fault into the Highlands. We don't want trouble.'

Layla thought of Duncan and Ewan, but it didn't deter her; she leapt from a branch and landed gracefully on her feet. She bounded through the trees with vibrations shooting through her. Feelings of elation erupted as she jumped in one swift, vertical movement and landed on a branch at the top of a towering fir tree. She listened intently as every sound blasted in her ears. The insects buzzed around the loch; the leaves rustled in the wind; the heartbeats pulsed in the small mammals running beneath her.

She heard a slow, drumming beat and, then, a whiff of the warm aroma caught in her nostrils; she could hear the liquid running through its veins. The appeal was not nearly as tempting as the girl passing the window earlier, but it would extinguish the flames that blazed in the back of her throat. She pounced ... darted ... soared and then pinned the deer to the woodland floor. Memories of her previous kill filled her mind as the deer thrashed about beneath her. Her lips opened, the two white incisors protruded and she stabbed deep and hard into its jugular. All her pent-up emotion poured into the feeding frenzy. After drinking the animal dry she wiped her mouth, jaws and neck. She could smell her aunt's distinctive smell and followed it to the edge of the reserve.

There were still so many effects of being an immortal Layla had to learn, but she felt more in command of her mind than ever before. The realisation of who she was bitter-sweet. A new ecosystem had developed in her mind and she had the choice to be at the top of it. Nonetheless she desperately hoped that her life as a vampire would not lead her to destroy someone like the attack she had witnessed in the city centre. The thought of the vampire reminded her of Regan and all her emotions merged. Anger about his lack of contact; greed as she thought of his sweet scent; lust, desire and passion as she imagined his touch; distress for his safety because of whom he'd gone away with.

13

Escape

Regan felt a surge of elation.

He and his 'brothers' were all running through the forest together. They were racing, as children would, as they swung from tree to tree and flew through the air. Regan discovered his capabilities instinctively. With Colleen gone, the freedom was a new experience for them all, although Daniel wasn't bothered either way.

'I can see every detail … This is amazing … I'll never need my glasses again!' Regan cried.

'There are some positive aspects to this. If only we didn't have the princess of doom dictating to us,' Padar said.

Daniel glared at him. But his scorn did not last long; he never had to compete with the other vampires while they hated Colleen.

They stopped at the top of the mountain and looked over the Glens.

'Wow!' Regan said, 'I've been blind; I can see people walking on the beach over in Scotland!'

A trigger went off in Jimmy's brain. He'd heard some of the other vampires talking about Scotland. He knew it was time to discuss his brother's future.

'Yeah, the scenery is unreal,' Daniel said.

'But you'll soon realise this is an awful existence. If it

didn't mean mass torture for the whole lot of us, I'd have disobeyed long ago,' Jimmy said.

He turned to the other vampires.

'Regan's my brother!' he suddenly confessed.

'Yeah bro!' Padar said, tapping Regan on the back.

'No,' Daniel said. 'That's not what he means.'

He knew exactly what Jimmy meant. Their resemblance was uncanny and he wondered how Colleen had not realised.

There was silence.

'What?' Padar said.

He was puzzled. Daniel should have known better; Padar had brought some of his dim wit with him from his fore-life.

'The lights are on but nobody's home,' Daniel said. 'You're supposed to be a vampire, vast brain and all that. He's his brother ... as in *human* brother.'

'Oh ... Oh ...!'

Jimmy nodded.

'Oh Jimmy ... I'm so sorry,' Padar said.

'No wonder you've been so quiet,' Daniel said, 'this must be a nightmare for you.'

'Yeah ... pretty much!' Jimmy said. 'When I saw his face I couldn't believe it. I had no idea she was looking for another mate. How hasn't she realised? She's usually so insightful. I swear if I could do something about her I would ...'

Regan interrupted. 'What are you on about? I've wanted to be able to sprint my whole life. Now I can fly, and see, like never before. I feel like I've got microscopic lenses attached to my eyes. I can hear every blade of grass move!'

Regan's joy was intense. He somersaulted through the air and landed crouched on his feet. He was very nimble and the others watched him with admiration.

'Regan, those things are just novelties ... You have no idea how terrible things can get here. Regan, you're a virgin,' Jimmy said bluntly.

'No I'm not!'

Regan gave Jimmy a look of scorn.

'That's why she changed you, Regan! She would never have taken another mate so quickly after Jimmy, if her hunters hadn't told her about you,' Padar said.

'Great ... now you're telling me you all know about my private life?' Regan said.

They all nodded.

'You are very valuable,' Padar said.

Regan frowned and then stared at him, confused.

Jimmy laughed. Regan attacked him as only a brother would. Daniel had to pry him off with the help of Padar.

'Sorry, Sullivan,' Jimmy said, calling him by his surname (the one they shared).

Regan growled. They all chuckled.

'What do you mean *hunters?*' he said.

'She hires them to find mates. There are two of them ... Kite and Franky ... I think that's what they're called,' Daniel said.

Regan fumed and kicked a rock. It flew into the air way out into the distance. They heard it crash, and then a sudden screeching of brakes as it hit a car. They all laughed; even Regan couldn't help himself.

'I am so gullible,' he said.

'That's what they do; they bait vampires for covens,' Jimmy said.

'If you stay here and she takes your virtue you'll be trapped,' Jimmy said.

'Good,' Regan said.

'No. Not good! You will belong to her and there is no escape. They torture vampires who try to escape,' Jimmy said.

'Well then ... I'd get tortured for trying to escape now,' Regan said.

'No, you wouldn't! She wouldn't be able to track you until she's had you because she can't sense you until then. We, however, are on her radar.'

'Isn't it the other way around? Don't I have her?' Regan said.

'You're as bad as Padar. Don't you understand what we're trying to tell you? While you're still a virgin, you're free,' Daniel said.

'Right, yeah, OK! I just don't get what the problem is,' Regan said.

'You won't until it's too late,' Daniel said. He was trying to convince Regan for his own gain.

'Where would I go? I don't know anyone,' Regan mused.

'I have a friend. He has a rebel vampire coven in Scotland. The vamps never go there. It's too dangerous for them,' Daniel said.

'Why? Surely we could overpower her together,' Regan asked.

'*She*'s not the problem! The Vamp Council is the problem! If they thought there was even talk of escape they would track us for as long as it took and punish us,' Daniel said.

'Regan … you *must* go,' Jimmy said.

'What about you? I just found you again. I can't leave you.'

'Yes you can. There's a better existence out there for you. You can carry on at university. Just make sure it's in Scotland,' he said.

Regan shuffled a little; he was unsure what to make of the whole situation. He would never have trusted the vampires had his brother not been one of them.

'I promise you,' Daniel said. 'You'll manage it. Colleen will blame herself for waiting too long … and she'll never tell the Council of your existence for fear of what they would do to her.'

'Give me your word, Regan. I *am* your older brother, and the more experienced vampire …' Jimmy smiled.

Regan growled.

'There's no need for that … I'll leave,' he said.

'Good, I'll take that as your word,' Jimmy said.

'I don't know that I'm so trustworthy anymore,' Regan said.

'You've only been a vampire five minutes – what would you know?' Jimmy laughed.

Regan swore to Jimmy that one day he would return. Jimmy didn't want to take any hope away from Regan and hugged him gratefully.

The vampires had agreed their plan of action. They thought it best Regan leave after Colleen's return since she would have no reason to question the other vampires about aiding his escape while she was with the coven. They knew Colleen would ask to see Regan soon and it was imperative they still threw her off guard. When Colleen returned home in the early hours of the morning Daniel knew she would be only too happy to be distracted by him. Of course she mentioned Regan, but he kept up the masquerade, knowing he would remain her most valuable mate once the new vampire had gone.

Regan seized the moment to sprint from the castle down to the shoreline. He could see the black rock that protruded out of the ocean perfectly; his vision illuminated its every detail in the dark. He leapt from the beach to the rock and landed squarely in the middle of it. He climbed into the boat that Padar had tied to the rock and began to row as fast as he could. He had little time to make his escape, but the boat moved across the water's surface as though it were being powered by an engine. His new-found athleticism astounded him. Hardly any time had elapsed before he reached the Scottish coastline and rowed the boat onto the sandy beach in front of him. He clambered out and sprinted up the shore, clutching the map Daniel had given him to go cross-country to Aberdeen.

Colleen was in the throes of passion with Daniel, oblivious to the escape, when Jimmy and Padar interrupted, just as they'd agreed. She knew immediately by their faces what had happened. She ran through the castle trying to find Regan's scent, but she knew it was pointless. Growling and sneering she returned to her three mates. They tried to avoid eye contact with her. She snarled with contempt.

'You said he was aggressive,' she roared.

'He was,' Daniel said.

'Shut up! *You* … speak!' Her voice roared as she grabbed Jimmy's arm.

Padar looked at Daniel. They had not anticipated she would be so angry, but they should have: she was unpredictable.

'Padar and I were hunting,' Jimmy stated simply.

Padar had never heard Jimmy so self-assured.

She reeled round on Daniel. 'Why did you entice me?' she sneered suspiciously. 'There's something about you I don't trust. I know you had something to do with this. Your hold on me is too intense.'

'I'm nothing but loyal to you, Colleen,' he said.

'You don't fear me; the other two do. Don't think I'm not aware of your confidence. If I find you had something to do with this, I will help to torture you myself.'

Her face fell as it dawned on her that she alone would be held responsible if word of this got out and in her mind, although she protested to the vampires, she thought she alone had allowed his escape – just as the vampires predicted she would. Daniel read her mind perfectly.

He sensed her rage changing when she started to blame herself. After all, she had no proof otherwise. Paddy and Jimmy glimpsed at him as he gave them an inconspicuous, reassuring nod. They were pleased; Jimmy was wary, but he didn't care, he would have sacrificed himself for Regan.

14

Q & A

Duncan knew.

Few were chosen to be Protectors of Scotland. Indeed, there were only three within the earthly realm. Duncan and Ewan were Frazer's protégés. He trained them, from childhood, in the way of the sword and gave them all the details they needed of their ancestry. As adults they swore their allegiance to Scotland and vowed to protect the people from their enemies.

Uncle Frazer spent a lot of time matchmaking; he pressed persistently for them to engage in the company of bonnie Scottish lassies. At first Duncan had wondered whether his uncle's animosity to Layla was just a case of bigotry, but now he had no doubt that his uncle was aware of Layla's identity. His uncle's possession of the Key to the Eternal Realm made him more powerful than he and Ewan put together. He also knew, however, that Ewan had no idea. The hunt had given him the evidence he needed to discover she was a vamp but Ewan had not seen it. Her naivety about her innate abilities had thrown him a red herring; she had not seemed to find anything wrong or odd in the kill. He thought he knew Layla inside out, and he'd been annoyed by Uncle Frazer's hostility toward her and felt protective of her. All this only confirmed to him that the old ghillie had known immediately what she

140

was. As a Highlander and Protector he knew her existence ought to outrage him, but as a man it made little difference. Layla had not acted oddly other than at the hunt and when he saw her in her splendour at the ceilidh his heart felt heavy.

Either he or Ewan would be given the Key to the Eternal Realm by Frazer. One had to prove himself worthy. The meaning of their entire existence had all been about training to become Protectors and she was an enemy of Scotland ... according to his ancestors. Duncan wondered if it was all a test for them. If so, he was failing miserably.

After Burns Night Duncan went to Aberdeen while Ewan and the girls returned to Glasgow. Whenever Ewan went to visit the girls, Duncan stayed in Aberdeen; he couldn't face seeing Layla. He had become a recluse; he no longer socialised or befriended girls as he did before. Ewan mentioned Layla's ill health and about how worried he felt. Duncan was certain Ewan would start to become suspicious if he did not snap himself out of his self-imposed isolation. He knew how loyal Ewan was to his heritage and how seriously he took his role so he said nothing to him of Layla. He feared Ewan's response. He had to speak to Layla, although he knew he may not like the answers to his questions. He had no idea how he would react if she confirmed what he was thinking, but he had to do it ... sooner rather than later.

He thought of the story of Drew Myntie, the powerful Scotsman of the early 1700s, convicted of murder by the then English ruler. He was hanged to death, as many of that time were, for a crime he claimed he never committed. Legend told that the black bile of his vengeance had transformed him into a vampire. His first victim was his own son, Cameron Myntie, and he, too, joined him in his vampire existence. Drew's bitter vengeance turned him into a cruel and vindictive beast. He turned further when his wife married another man and he began to savage and enslave young girls.

141

His entire existence was based on revenge. He punished his wife by forcing his son to take her as his first victim.

Drew Myntie's identity remained hidden in the murky shadows for hundreds of years until he preyed on a Highlander's daughter. Frazer, the only Highlander in the earthly realm at that time, had to summon the other Highlanders back to execute Drew Myntie but his son Cameron escaped to Ireland. No one knew for a very long time that Cameron Myntie had returned to Scotland. He lived under a pseudonym, Myntie McIntosh, his mother's maiden name, and he had a beautiful young wife. They lived quietly in the Highlands of Scotland until Myntie's heritage caught up with him. He could not help but take his wife, Briege, and then her younger sister, Colleen. Unfortunately it was never enough for him and he began to take more vamps and created a coven.

It was when he took a protégé and brought him over from Belgium that the Highlanders caught wind of the situation. Frazer had to summon them again to help him bring an end to Myntie's acts of terror. The Highlanders made one fatal error, however; they released the vamps instead of executing them and they merely replicated their master's example. To avenge their suffering they transformed into self-professed persecutors of men. Nonetheless the Highlanders and the vamps made an agreement that they, the vampires, would never inhabit Scotland again and so the Highlanders had no reason to involve themselves in the activities of the vamps in other countries. His protégé, Joubert Popper, fled to Bruges, where he took a vamp named Amara. When he found true love with a second vamp, he set Amara free, and the couple vanished. Thereafter the Vamp Council HQ was in Bruges, the Dead City. The Council held their meetings in a sanctum hidden below the belfry in the centre of the city.

*   *   *

Duncan performed his usual drumming rap on Layla's door.

Please, Duncan thought, don't be a vamp; they will want to eliminate you and I know you aren't my enemy.

He waited for her to open the door. She peaked round the barely open door and met his wary gaze. The familiar strapping man stared at her while she sparkled before him.

'Hello,' she sang.

'Aye … hello,' he said. His voice was breaking and crackling with nerves.

'Come in,' she said.

He walked behind her in silence. The house was empty and she led him into the living room.

'Sit down,' she gestured.

'No, I'd rather stand, thanks,' he said.

'OK.'

'I have something to ask you.'

'OK.'

He hesitated. The beads of sweat gathered on his brow.

'Are you a vamp?'

'No.'

'No … What do you mean, no?'

'No, I'm not a vamp.'

'Oh right! Well what are you then?'

'A vampeire,' she said. 'That's V-A-M-P-*E*-I-R-E,' she added merrily.

Silence filled the room

'So you are a vamp. I don't appreciate you winding me up.'

'I'm not a vamp.'

'So what exactly is it?'

'It's not *it* – it's *me*.'

'So you're a vampire.'

'No! Why do you always have to be so argumentative?'

He stepped back, nervous.

'And what are you stepping back for, you lunatic. I'm not going to bite,' she laughed.

'That's not funny, Layla!'

He felt more confused. He recognised her humour; she didn't seem different. She looked glowing but then she'd always been stunning to him.

'I'm part human, my mother was human but yes I am part vamp. My father, I've never met him, was a vampire, Connor Eire. Remember, I've been a Vampeire since birth; I'm still Layla!'

Duncan looked at her slightly bemused.

'Are you a Highlander?' she asked.

'Um … ah … um.'

'It's a simple yes or no answer.'

'Yes,' he said.

He bowed his head slightly.

'You're still Duncan. So now we can see each other for what we really are: powerful freaks.'

He looked into her eyes. They were hypnotic, but he still recognised her. He laughed heartily and it felt like he hadn't laughed for years.

'You do realise we are immortal enemies?'

'Ewan already thought that when we thought each other mortal.'

She paused and looked at him with as much sincerity as she could muster.

'I'm not a killer, Duncan. I'm not a vegetarian but I *am* part-human. Here …' she said.

She grabbed his hand and put it to her breast.

'See, my heart beats,' she said.

Her heart was so slow and faint; his pounded. It felt like it might jump out of his chest. He didn't want to move his hand from her breast. He gulped.

'You are the only one who knows about that,' she said.

Duncan looked at her. Guilt wore it's own look!

'I'm as confused as you, Duncan; I seem to swap between the two forms. I can do anything I put my mind to but it does not interfere with me as a human.'

'Nothing new there then!'

She smiled.

'It's a little different.'

'Aye ... I know that already! If your hunting was anything to go by, I can only imagine what you mean.'

'Have you made your decision?'

For a moment he was puzzled, then it dawned on him that she must have been eavesdropping on the night of the ceilidh.

'You heard!' He was a little shocked.

'Yeah ... I didn't mean to; I got lost in the house.'

Duncan laughed.

'I've been going there my whole life and I still get lost.'

'Obviously I still have a lousy sense of direction,' Layla chuckled.

He laughed loud.

'You made my decision for me; but I'm only one vote, Layla. I'm not so sure about telling Ewan yet.'

'I know ... Maybe we could try a little normality for as long as it lasts.'

'I need a bit of time to get my head round all of this. Maybe we could go out for your eighteenth.'

'OK great, there's a band playing in Ashton Lane, they're from Aberdeen. I've heard they're pretty good.'

She stood up and Duncan backed away.

'Sorry,' she said.

He smiled and she leaned in and grabbed him.

'Ow!' he said.

'Oops, I forget my strength,' she chuckled.

She hugged him more gently and thanked him. She kissed him on the cheek. He flinched at first, but then when he could smell her scent in his nose he held her tightly. He blushed. He was glad he towered above her; his feelings overwhelmed him but at least she couldn't see his face.

'I'll call you,' he said.

'Yeah, thanks.'

15

Lost and Found

Regan arrived in Aberdeen in the early hours. He was free …
at least in so far as a vampire could ever be.

He knocked on the apartment door and a young, pale,
red-haired male opened the door. He was dressed like he was
about to charge at English troops, minus the spear and
shield. His hair fell over his shoulders in tails. He wore a kilt
and a white T-shirt.

'Hi,' he said.

He extended his hand.

'Regan … right!'

'Were you expecting me?' Regan asked.

'Aye … there are many ways and means in our existence,'
he said.

Regan could detect the sarcasm in his voice. He laughed,
'The joy of text!'

He laughed louder. Regan smiled.

'Come on in out of the cold,' he said.

Regan stepped into the apartment.

'I'm Graham. All my mates call me Gray.'

Regan's face fell. The word 'mate' had new connotations
for him.

'Sorry … I meant friends.'

Regan relaxed.

'Did you think you'd jumped out of the frying pan into the fire? Not the best idea for a vampire!' Gray laughed.

'Yeah, something to that effect,' he said.

Gray led Regan through to the sitting room. As he entered he noticed a full drum kit sitting in one corner of the room. Nearby stood three people. There were two males, one with dark hair and one with fair; they had strong facial features that shone in the moonlight as it beamed through the window. The fourth was a female but she seemed different.

'I wasn't expecting to see a vamp,' he mused.

'A vamp ... this one? She's more tramp than vamp; much as she'd like to be,' Gray laughed.

Regan was puzzled. Then he smelt the sweet aroma. She was human.

'Oh ... no...!' he said. He ran from the room.

Gray followed him.

'It's your first?' he asked.

'Yeah,' Regan said.

'I'm surprised how contained you were. I thought we were going to have to restrain you. Let me get you something to drink to ease the craving. Did you hunt on the way here?' he asked.

Regan shook his head.

Gray pulled a live chicken from the laundry room and handed it to Regan.

'If you made it cross-country to the Granite City without killing anyone you'll be fine with Cara.'

'Granite City?'

'Aka Aberdeen,' Gray said.

'Oh ... I see. I thought it was a special vampire name. I'm still learning. I didn't risk stopping in case I did succumb to anything.'

Gray laughed.

'I heard you're pretty new to all of this. You're doing really well. Here have a wee dram; the alcohol helps to confuse your senses. I tend to stay on the sauce most of the time, that way my senses think a rat is lean cuisine.'

Regan laughed. He wondered if that was why Kite and Franky drank so much. He winced at the thought of them and their treachery.

'Don't listen to him, Regan,' one of the tall, dark-haired vampires said.

'Gray tries that trick with everyone. The alcohol is, as with most things in this existence, very, very fast-acting.'

Gray laughed in the background.

Regan followed Gray back into the living room and set down his glass on a small table as he walked past it. He remembered the destructiveness of alcohol in his human life. Blood was enough of an addiction for him without adding another to the list.

'What's with your accent?' Regan said. 'Mine is indistinct now. Your accent is so strong. I thought there were no covens in Scotland.'

'There aren't. I was backpacking round Europe when I got nabbed. We've been here a long time … By the way, this is Cam, Derek and Cara.'

'Hi!'

Regan waved, keeping his distance.

'Sorry about the entrance,' he said.

'That's no bother at all; Cara's used to it,' Cam said.

He had a Scottish accent too. 'Were you a shoemaker in your human life?' Regan quipped.

'Are you calling me a snob?' Cam laughed.

'Cam, Derek and I were in the same coven. Our vamp was executed. We don't know why, but then we never gave a fiddlers and made our escape when we got the chance. Oh, and Cara here, she very cleverly worked out what we were. That's why we don't hide from her. She's a good mate, but thankfully not in a malevolent way. She's our manager.'

'It's a pleasure to meet you all,' he said.

He was unsure why a rebel coven needed a manager.

'Likewise,' they replied.

'Daniel said there were four of you but he never mentioned a girl.'

'Oh, there *are* four. Our English buddy, Ollie. He just left to pick up our wages.'

'Right,' Regan said.

He was getting more confused by the second.

'I'll show you to your room. Obviously some of us have to share; there's not much privacy here. We thought you might like a room on your own for a while. I'm sure Daniel told you we move around a lot. It keeps us inconspicuous,' Gray said.

He steered Regan in the direction of a small room at the end of the hall. There was little more than a bed and a chair.

'I appreciate this,' Regan said.

'Don't worry; you'll have to earn your keep.'

Regan looked over at him, baffled.

'When you're ready come back to the other room.'

Regan slumped into the chair. He'd not had time to think about what happened, who he was or if he had a future, but then he didn't suppose anything would ever feel settled again. It felt more intense than but not unlike his move into halls in Glasgow. He'd left his other life behind then; the only difference was his awkward appetite for blood. The expansion of his brain was remarkable. He would have an eternity to fill it with knowledge. People dreamed of immortality but perhaps that was because they did not realise how long that would be and the loneliness that came with it. He could smell the girl in the other room. The price of forever could be costly to her or him.

He could hear them talking.

'It must be daunting for him,' Gray was saying. 'The transformation usually takes a while to get used to and he's had to go into hiding straight away. Plus he hasn't dipped his wick yet,' Gray chuckled.

Regan could even feel Cara's displeasure as she glared at

Gray. He re-entered the room and noticed how the vampires kept an invisible barrier in front of Cara. Was he so unpredictable? He told himself again and again that he would never touch a human.

'How you feeling, mate?' Gray asked.

'Strange, confused, like I'm in a whirlpool.'

Cam smiled reassuringly. 'But you do seem to be choosing your conscience.'

Another vampire came into the room.

'Awright, mate? I'm Ollie,' he said, offering his hand.

'Things can never be as bad as they are for Ollie,' Gray quipped. 'Imagine being English in Scotland and a vampire on top of that.'

Cam rolled with laughter and the others joined in.

'I'm ever so popular as you can imagine,' Ollie rejoined.

Regan laughed.

'So, do you play any instruments?' the dark-haired vampire said in a soft Scottish accent. He spoke for the first time.

Regan looked at him totally bemused. 'Instruments?'

'Aye ... *musical* instruments,' Derek explained.

'No. I'm tone deaf,' he said.

'Reality check ... not anymore; you should have pretty good hearing now,' Derek pointed out.

'We have plenty of time to teach you. Is there anything you always wanted to play? Or can you sing?' Cam asked.

'I was thrown out of the school glee club,' Regan chuckled.

'You look happy enough to me, old chap.' Ollie asked.

Regan shook his head gently.

'Glee club is like choir,' Gray laughed. 'Cara's our lead singer; we could use a male vocalist,' he added.

Cam positioned himself at the drums.

'I play bass, Ollie plays lead and bonnie Cara sings. She can play sax too. Cara can really belt out the ballads.' Gray said.

'Do you want to try a duet, Regan?' Cara asked.

Regan had no idea why he agreed to try out. Cara had a

sweet, girly voice. He processed their forms and voices and tried to convince himself it was a good idea to sing.

'The band is our cover,' Gray said.

'The shifts suit us, and the dark is always the safer option,' Ollie added.

'We fit in perfectly here. It's our Highlander friends we have to avoid so we don't bother biting chickens heads off on stage,' Cam mocked.

'Isn't Scotland safe?' Regan questioned.

'Yes it is, but there are a few locals we have to dodge. They don't like us much. In fact, to them I am the devil himself,' Ollie said.

'Ah ... an *English* vampire,' Regan chuckled.

'You got it, old chap!'

'This is the most northerly we would venture and we never go above Glasgow on the west coast. We're unsure exactly where they live so we avoid the Highlands altogether,' Gray explained.

'Who are they?' Regan asked.

'They are the reason no vamps ever come here. They are the Highlanders. There are only a few, but they are dangerous shapeshifters,' answered Derek.

'Cara is our eyes and ears, being the Scottish lass locals are more forthcoming with info to her,' Gray said.

'OK,' Regan said.

He turned to listen to Cara who spoke in a small voice.

'A Highlander's daughter was once killed by a vampire; that's all I know.'

Jimmy had never mentioned the Highlanders but everyone seemed very calm and preferred their life in Scotland to being with a vamp.

'So ... what would you like to sing, Regan?' Cara asked.

'She's got the mind of a vampire; she can change from one subject to another without flinching,' Derek laughed.

'Um ... I know the American national anthem!'

They all laughed.

'Thought you might … Why not then?' Cara said.

Regan started singing and they slowly joined in with their instruments. To his own surprise, he really could sing – his voice was strong and low – and they were all delighted; he was just what they needed. Regan stopped and the room fell silent. He had never been able to sing before; he couldn't understand where his velvet voice had come from. He knew the words to 'Bridge over Troubled Water' so he sang again. Cara improvised and joined in; and when they'd finished, they tried it again.

'You *can* sing, old chap!'

'Yeah,' Regan grinned and realised why they needed a manager.

The band was called Summerland and Regan took on the role of lead vocalist. Cara lined up a few gigs and their life was on the road as travelling musicians. Regan fitted like a final piece of the jigsaw. They roamed the Scottish Lowlands, flitting between Aberdeen, Edinburgh and Dundee, and through the towns and villages around the cities. Regan felt as though he was living a dream, especially when Daniel phoned Gray to let him know Jimmy and the coven were safe. Ollie spent endless hours teaching Regan to play guitar and he practised endlessly, although he knew it would take time to perfect his sound. He wanted the set to include him playing acoustic guitar and singing.

One night during a rehearsal Cara and Cam started arguing.

'For goodness' sake, Cam; I'm as good as a vampire. I live with you. I'm an honorary vampire; why not just make me one?'

Cara wanted nothing more than to be a vampire and one of them, but they had all long ago agreed it was not an option. They had all experienced the wrath of vamps and

Cara was the most wonderful human; she was too precious to risk changing. She had the heart of an angel and none of them wanted to stop it from beating. That aside, none of them wanted to taste human blood again.

'Cara, we've been over this a hundred times. Apart from the safety aspect, and the fact that you might turn into a raving lunatic, we need you! You are our chief negotiator. Scotland has been good to us. Why would we alert the Highlanders to our presence when we've had a peaceful existence for so long?'

'I'm furious,' she said.

Cam, Derek and Ollie laughed loudly. Cara had no idea what fury meant.

'So you see, you could turn into a heartless vamp and destroy us all,' Gray said.

'You're so selfish. You know I love you all,' Cara said.

'As we love you, but you don't want this existence. Always looking over your shoulder, never being sure what the future holds is a curse, a torment. If we were caught you would not suffer at a Highlander's hand, because you're human!' Cam said.

'Regan, please,' she said, turning to him with pleading eyes.

'Don't involve me,' he said. His answer was final.

She begged. It damaged them to say no to her, but it was with the best intentions.

'Cara,' Derek said, 'Regan has not even tasted human blood. How would you expect him to stop? What you're asking is not fair and we vowed never to cause another human fatality; we don't know if we would have the power to stop. It's why we have chosen animal blood. Do you know the demons we fight inside to abstain from touching you? You're tempting us.'

'I know, I'm sorry; I know your moral standing on it all. It's just I don't want to get old while you all stay thirty for ever.'

'Hey … I'm still young. Don't have me as old as this lot,' Regan said.

'We may be older but at least we're not virgins,' Cam laughed.

'And you're ugly but we can't all be perfect,' Regan jibed.

'Give it a rest,' Cara snapped, 'you *all* look good.'

'How many more times, girl? We see what's inside. The beauty is in your soul and that will never age. If you became a vamp, you'd lose your soul for good …' Ollie said.

She hugged Ollie.

'If you didn't have a soul you would have killed me and thousands more,' she said, and let the subject drop.

It was Saturday night and their first time gigging in Glasgow. The gig was in Ashton Lane, near the university, so they knew it would draw a crowd and fill the venue. The atmosphere was always cracking with plenty of revellers. Cara joined the crowd when Regan sang solo. He always sounded like he was serenading someone personally. There was such honesty behind his voice and girls fell in love with him when he sang. That night it felt even more intimate as if he were connecting with someone in the audience. Even Regan was perplexed by his emotion. After the gig they packed up their band kit and Cara went to the van to collect a rucksack for the leads.

Regan recognised her instantly. Ever since his transformation he'd had someone inside his head, just a figure, an outline, and he finally realised who fitted it when he saw her. He could smell her fragrant scent. It stimulated his feelings and he remembered now how he felt when he had kissed her.

He approached her but even before he reached her she turned her head. She was like a porcelain doll as she moved in slow motion; her blonde tresses sweeping over her face and the familiar emerald eyes glinting; he could hear the soft flutters of her heart.

155

'Hello, Layla,' he crooned.

She nodded to him and turned her head away again. He expected no less. He had not contacted her and he could understand her animosity. She turned back sharply; she recognised the eyes.

The eyes were Regan's but they were different. She scanned his form as she saw how solid he was. It was something no one else would have noticed. His voice, his American accent was unrecognisable. She questioned whether it was him when she listened to how different he sounded but the eyes were unmistakeable. How had she not recognised him until that point?

Suddenly she became aware of Duncan and Ewan in the background and she hid her recognition of him. If he was a vampire he would hear her inaudible voice when she asked him to leave her alone. She knew he would think she wanted nothing to do with him, but she had no choice. Duncan and Ewan would not see what he was, but Duncan was too perceptive of her emotions. Regan turned and walked away when her muted tones reached him. He looked back and then lowered his gaze. She was right. His leaving confirmed her suspicions and her heart fluttered gently; he glanced back once more.

The cobbled street was filled with utility vans. They had had to park their van on Byers Road, a trek with all their kit for humans but not a big deal for them. Cara had not returned from the van so the rest of the band gathered up the kit and went to meet her.

Regan had the leads while the others carried the instrument cases and speakers. They walked as casually as they could. They could hear the lingering heartbeats; see the fondling in corners and sense the inebriated souls, in doorways, all unaware of them.

Ahead of them, by their van, they spotted a figure leaning over a prostrate form. It was Cara.

'Stop!' Gray suddenly shouted.

The others dropped their cases and sprinted. It was just as well the humans around them were too engrossed in their own antics to recognise what was happening.

'Call an ambulance!' Gray bellowed.

Derek reached Cara first and cradled her in his arms, but her heart had already stopped. He tried biting into each wrist. He shook her, but she was lifeless. Gray stopped him from trying to immortalise her further. They let her go in peace. None of them could save her, it was too late.

Regan stood up; he saw the figure flash in the distance. He flew, and chased, matching the speed and agility of the other form. And then, he saw her swoop down and glance at him as she crossed the threshold into her home. He stopped. The horror masked his face when he recognised the door, just as he'd recognised her form.

Cara never had any family. Her mother had died when she was thirteen and her father, a drunk, threw her out on the street when she was sixteen. Regan related to her, even in his transformation. Sometimes he pitied her but he knew it was not his place to offer her the existence he had embraced. The vampires had given Cara solace from an abusive life and expected nothing from her in return. She had become their sister and the enormity of the pain had a gravitational pull on all of them. Every tiny line on her twenty-five-year-old face had disappeared and she lay smooth, cold and ashen; the figure of a vampire, everything she longed to be, but silent. They had not granted her the immortality she yearned for, but she had something better: she had peace, something they could not imagine.

Back in the Granite City the vampires packed their instruments away and took menial jobs to pay the rent. The apartment was silent and often empty.

Derek appeared in the room where Regan stood at the

window. Despite the deep darkness the granite of the city's buildings seemed to be alive, glinting like silver.

'You OK, Regan?' Derek said.

'Yeah.'

'You seem a bit distracted.'

Regan laughed. 'When are we ever *not* distracted?'

'Aye … true.'

'It's a nightmare sometimes. The vamps took all our hopes and dreams away from us. There are so many things we will never get to experience,' Regan fumed.

'Like …'

'I don't know. There are so many things: life, marriage, children … love!'

'Aye,' Derek sighed.

They were silent again. Derek watched Regan intently.

'What brought this on?'

'I don't know!'

'We can still have love, you know!'

Regan looked at him, perplexed, but Derek's gaze never faltered.

'It's dangerous to love but it was out of my control. I loved Cara.'

'I know! We all did.'

'No Regan … I *really* loved Cara,' Derek said.

He turned to look at Regan and met his gaze. And it was then that Regan registered what he meant.

'Oh. Derek, I'm so sorry.'

Regan felt unnerved, guilty.

'When we met Cara, I fell in love with her immediately. We all agreed that she could not be told what we were. But Cara, being Cara, worked it out pretty quickly. I never had the courage to tell her, but I could sense the feelings were mutual. Telling her would only have made her want to change more. Loving her meant I had to let her go. She was family to me.'

'I know.'

158

'Regan, I will never love anyone again. My heart went with her and sometimes I want to find the Highlanders so I can end it all. Only it would put the rest of my brothers in danger. I warn you the heartache is unbearable.'

'I can't say I know how you must feel. But would you have chosen never to feel for Cara, never to feel love?'

'We have free will to choose. That was given to you when you escaped from Colleen Duffy, but sometimes feelings find you. I think this heartache is better than feeling nothing at all. It was worth every second with Cara.'

'I thought our natural instinct was to feel lust and desire, not love?'

'I assure you my feelings were not lust. I don't deny I wanted Cara but I was never sure if it was her blood or her love I craved, until I held her bleeding in my arms.'

Derek left the room but Regan did not move. He heard Derek leave the flat. He wondered why Derek had chosen to tell him such deep feelings. It helped him to make his decision. When Derek glanced up at him from the street below Regan nodded.

Getting them all together was not an easy feat. They all seemed to want to spend their time alone.

'Go on, Regan … we won't bite,' Derek laughed.

His comments warmed the chilly atmosphere.

'You might want to … when I've said what I have to say,' Regan said.

He furrowed his brow.

'For goodness' sake, Regan, spit it out. We don't have all the time in the world,' Cam guffawed.

The others were rolling about the floor. He hadn't heard them laugh since Cara died.

'Well, there *are* four of you and just one of me.'

They all laughed at the prospect of attacking him. He was silent, trying to work out whether or not he should tell them what he knew about Cara's death.

'I've decided to spend some time on my own,' Regan said.

He thought it might have been too much for them to bear.

'Of course I would like your agreement, since I am still very young and inexperienced.'

Derek already knew why Regan was leaving. He'd never mentioned his intuitive gift to the other vampires. Regan seemed to have a conscience; Derek had never seen such focus. The other vampires, even after seventy years of a human-free diet, were still more unpredictable than he.

'You'll be fine, Regan,' Derek said.

Cam looked at Gray; Gray looked at Derek; Ollie looked at Cam; Cam looked at Derek.

'You are very even tempered,' Gray said.

'My mind is tormented, but no more than when my heart was beating,' Regan said.

'I think you have the most developed sense of right and wrong I've ever seen in this soulless existence,' Ollie said.

'I was not always a veggie!' Gray said.

Regan listened to him intently.

'When you drink mortal blood,' Gray went on, 'you gain strength and youth. All feelings of righteousness get lost as you become addicted to the essence. I fight the craving daily, and I have done for the last seventy years. Some days are so tough I wonder how I keep myself sane but you seem to have a natural ability to abstain. You don't seem to struggle at all,' Gray said.

Regan knew they had all, at some point, given in to the pull of mortal blood but he never expected such honesty.

'I *do* struggle but it's inside,' he said.

'We all do,' Gray said.

'Cara was probably taken by a hunter passing through. It could have been the same hunters who work for Colleen,' Cam said.

Regan knew better but decided to keep silent.

'Cara hasn't been the only victim recently. We heard of a

similar incident in Glasgow. It was a little different to Cara's killing; it happened in broad daylight. That's very unusual for a vampire – firstly, to take such a risk of being identified, and secondly, to walk about in daylight so freely. Only those who have found their protection can do such things,' Gray said.

'I still don't risk daylight hours, even though I found this ring from my previous life. I remember the burning sensation too well when I stood in sunlight unprotected,' Cam noted.

Regan's jaw dropped. No one had mentioned being able to walk freely in daylight. It made him wonder what would protect him but his mind soon flitted when he saw Derek staring at him. It was as if Derek could visualise the ever-turning visions of Layla in his mind. Again his mind changed. How had Layla become such a monster?

'You should do what feels right for you, nipper,' Ollie said.

Regan could hear his friends' words droning in and out in the background. He needed to find Layla before the Highlanders discovered what she was, for all their sakes.

'Take care, Regan,' Derek said.

He took Regan's hand in a firm grip and pulled him in tight, patting his back.

'You know where we are if you need us,' Derek added.

'I will. I'll be careful not to give the Highlanders any reason to find us.'

They all nodded.

16

Second Chances

After Layla's eighteenth Ewan and Duncan returned to Aberdeen and she was relieved; hiding the horror of the night had been difficult, especially keeping it from Duncan. She had no choice; accepting her had been enough of a challenge for him; evidence of another vampire, and its more vicious activities, would only have incensed him. It could have caused him to inform Ewan and Uncle Frazer prematurely, resulting in a Highlander intervention.

Layla pored over the details of the attack as she tried to comprehend how she hadn't recognised Leon sooner. She'd shirked his company so often that inviting him along to her birthday celebrations had seemed the right thing to do. She never imagined he could have been such a beast.

She retraced the events in her memory. The restaurant had been quiet, and she had been a little testy. She remembered each intricate detail of her conversation with Leon.

'I'm looking forward to this evening,' Leon said.

He was animated and bright.

'Yeah,' she sighed. She had almost instantly regretted inviting him to her birthday outing. She couldn't imagine how he and Duncan and Ewan would get on; they were chalk and cheese. Well, it was too late now.

'Layla, your eyes are really dark; your pupils have almost covered your iris,' Leon said.

She shuffled in her chair.

'I've been really tired. It could be the medication I've been taking,' she said. She hoped it would throw him off course.

'I don't mean to be nosy, but you're *really* pale.'

Layla shuffled again; he seemed to notice everything. She wondered if maybe inviting him out had been the wisest idea. She was finding him extremely irritating, and his comments always seemed to have some covert meaning behind them.

'Layla, I'm not hitting on you; I'm not that way inclined,' he assured her.

Two thoughts entered her head. Firstly, how did he know what she had been thinking? Secondly, there was only one type of man she knew that could be so intuitive about women.

'You're gay,' she blurted out.

'Aye,' he laughed.

'Only a gay man could notice a girl being a bit off colour; or a man who was in love with you, so I knew it was one or the other. I bet on the other,' she said.

'You're very perceptive. I did think at one point I might be attracted to you, but then I realised it was envy.'

Layla stared at him. He did not see her as female or male; simply as a being.

'Why would you envy me?' she asked. She wondered how anyone would want the chaos of the inner demons she possessed.

'I'm just superficial!' he grinned.

'No one ever knows everybody completely,' she said.

Leon stared at her, puzzled for a moment. 'Ooh … that's deep. It's as well we're going out tonight. You really need to lighten up.'

Layla wondered whether she could ever 'lighten up'

again. Her craving for blood would not subside. Orange juice or caffeine would have to suffice until she hunted after work.

She met Leon, as arranged, outside the Metro station on Byers Road. They were meeting Duncan, Ewan and the girls in the pub. Leon had a friend with him and he introduced him as Raj. The swarthy-skinned man was much taller and leaner than Leon. He extended his hand.

'Hi,' she said.

'That's a firm handshake,' he said.

She smiled, reminding herself to loosen her grip in future. She examined Raj. She'd not imagined him to be the type of man Leon would date. He, Leon, was … superficial; it had been Leon's own word. Raj looked older and intelligent. He looked distinguished with a few grey hairs and his glasses were not top-of-the-range designer. He and Leon seemed complete opposites, but that was so often the case with … lovers?

'Have you and Leon been friends long?' she asked Raj.

Silence. She assumed he hadn't heard her. Raj did seem half asleep but Leon jumped in with an answer, confirming they'd known one another a while.

Layla introduced Leon and Raj to her friends as they entered the pub. The girls thought Leon was hilarious and rolled with laughter when he jested and joked with them. Duncan and Ewan dodged him, behaving like homophobes. Until the ceilidh in Inverness, Layla had always believed they were open-minded, but their behaviour there had caused her to have a rethink. Raj sat in a daze at the bar most of the night. He was more interested in the liquor than the company. She'd given up trying to make conversation with him. The band started at ten. Layla spent her time between Leon and the girls and Duncan and Ewan.

She remembered Regan approaching her. She had been transfixed when she noticed what he had transformed into but she dared not react. She thought he'd lost interest in her. The two Highlanders had her in view so communicating was a bad idea. He would definitely have put himself, and possibly her, in danger.

As he walked away she felt the familiar draw to him she had forgotten existed, and a fresh image of him was seared into her mind, just as before. She enjoyed the yearning he stimulated in her. At first it was a similar sensation to being parched and thinking of him quenched it, but then it became more intense. The hint of his sweet scent lingered in the air; she wished she could taste it to calm her senses.

Soon after Layla left the pub with Duncan and Ewan; they couldn't stomach Leon further. The night air, or the alcohol, hit them; suddenly they were vocalising their views of him. They agreed he was an arrogant, conceited little parasite and they never wanted to be in his company again. The constant talking was giving Layla a head rush. She didn't find Leon *that* bad; he was sometimes a little irritating, but not horrid.

But it was that very moment that at last she realised what Leon was. How had he taken her so long? Shivers ran up her spine; she quivered at the thought of what might have happened had Ewan and Duncan discovered that he was not only gay, but a vampire too. Two revelations in one night; it seemed unreal. Her mind seemed to be playing tricks with her again and her imagination was running wild. It seemed as if everyone that she knew had transformed into some fantastical character.

Duncan and Ewan left Layla at her door. As she watched them leave, she felt a powerful force pulling her back to Ashton Lane. She sensed imminent danger and fled in a whirl of dust. She slowed to a brisk walk in keeping with her human form. She scanned the alleyways and pathways that branched off the lane; her legs seemed to be moving automatically. Now she was in Byers Road, and in her fore-vision she could see a white van parked along the kerb. Leon was sitting inside beside the pretty singer from the band and initially Layla assumed he was kissing Cara's hand. But when her nose picked up the sweet smell of fresh blood, and her eyes saw it trickle down the girl's neck, she thought differently.

Subconsciously she licked her lips but the sight of Leon's fangs jolted her back to reality. She sprinted towards him but already he'd sprung away from the van and flown up into the air. For an instant she met his gaze and scowled. Then she hesitated: should she pursue him or save the girl? She pulled Cara from the car and laid her on the footpath, desperately trying to distract herself from the compulsive scent, that was stirring her thirst for Cara's blood. She focused on the slow heart rate, barely audible, and when it fell silent she knew it was too late. Her injuries were to her jugular, just as with the sprite, but there was a further bite mark on her wrist. Layla tried to stop the bleeding, just as Megan had for the old drunk. Layla rubbed Cara's brow and whispered reassuring words and tried to ease her passing. The girl spluttered and blood sprayed from her mouth.

'Der … ek,' she cried, and then gasped. Her heart fluttered. It stopped. Final.

Regan and the other band members appeared from out of the alleyway. She contemplated keeping her ground, but when they dashed forward she darted away as her human fear took hold.

She soared through the air, tears running down her face. She seemed to have no idea about anything. It felt the same as the night she had discovered Duncan and Ewan's identity. How had she missed Leon's silent soul? How could she have been so gullible? He was heartless but she could not condemn his instincts; she had enough trouble controlling her own.

As she reached Kate's home, she briefly saw Regan's face,

passing in front of her like a bright shadow. In that instant she knew that Regan had condemned her, that he accused her of an unspeakable crime.

She wiped the bloody tears from her face and stepped over the threshold of her front door.

17

Glasgow Kiss

Regan waited outside the restaurant every evening, but she never appeared. He spent the dark hours, after it closed, hunting or in the casino. He had no aversion to risk and no need for sleep; the reverse of his human life. His conflicting thoughts had followed him too; he could not control them so he existed by distraction. To repel the scent of the humans crossing his path, he used the money he earned from gigging with the band and frequented some local casinos (he had lost all his savings when his accounts were closed after his 'accidental death' in Glenarm). He found a talent for counting cards and developed an addiction for blackjack. It did not curb his conflict; it was just another vice. Sometimes he tried to avoid gambling and went hunting to relieve the aggression he felt and to stunt his compulsive gambling habit. It didn't work; he became very wealthy, very quickly. He started to find it increasingly difficult to gain entry to casinos in the Glasgow area so he ventured further afield, sometimes to Edinburgh and Dundee.

One night, as he paced outside the restaurant on the other side of the road he noticed the waiter who'd been in the restaurant that first day he'd met Layla; he'd been at the gig in Ashton Lane with Layla, too. He began to cross the road, intending to ask if he knew when she would be back.

Something stopped him in his tracks. He suddenly saw the tall dark figure before him for what he was and saw the blankness in the restaurant window behind him. Had he been the one who had changed Layla? He was filled with sudden fury. Regan saw Leon's eyes widen as he caught sight of Regan, and Regan turned away quickly to calm himself. Suddenly he realised that he was in the middle of the road. and he dodged an oncoming car, its beeping horn ringing in his ears. When he looked back across the road, the man had gone inside. Was this vampire the reason why Layla had not returned? Yes, he was sure of it. He decided to wait for closing.

When the restaurant was clear of customers and staff, and the vampire was on his own, Regan darted through the door. Leon had been expecting him. He recognised him from the pub and had been watching him pacing outside the restaurant for weeks. He only appeared at dusk, which was a dead giveaway. Leon crouched, holding his position as he sensed Regan's rage. Regan growled and hissed through his clenched teeth.

'I'm much older, stronger and wiser than you, I assure you,' Leon snarled.

'I think I might be willing to take that chance,' Regan roared.

'So this is not about Layla?' Leon said.

His tone was even and Regan immediately stood upright.

'How do you know why I'm here?' Regan asked.

'Something tells me you've not been hanging around to gawp at me. The anger in your eyes tells me the only kiss you may be thinking of giving me is a Glasgow kiss,' Leon sniggered.

Regan puckered his brow; Leon was speaking in riddles.

'You're trying to discover what happened to the young girl who was a member of your band,' Leon said.

Regan crouched; snarled and readied himself to pounce.

169

'I'm stating fact, vampire,' Leon growled.

Regan stood up again.

'I told you I'm older and I'd have you before you reached here. I also have some of the answers you may be looking for. For one, I tried to save your friend by trying to transform her. Next time I won't bother, and there *will* be a next time. There are hunters here, but I'm not one of them. I've abstained from drinking the mortal drug by killing someone for over seventy of my hundred years, so being in her presence was a difficult choice for me. It was too late; she had already been bled dry,' Leon added.

'Was it Layla?'

'No!'

'I saw her with Cara and she ran when we were approaching her,' Regan said.

'She thinks I killed her. She saw me biting the girl's wrist but it was too late,' Leon stated.

'But Layla ran ...'

'I told you. There are hunters, but I assure you Layla is not one of them.'

'Did you see who killed her?'

'Well ... yes and no,' Leon said.

Regan shook his head and put his head in his hands and then lifted it again.

'Male or female?' he asked.

'What with all the flowing locks these days, and with girls wearing the same clothes, it's kind of hard to distinguish,' Leon said.

Leon looked away and then turned back.

'We all move with the same speed and grace and I will admit that I thought it was Layla too ... at first. But the horror on her face was all the proof I needed,' he said.

'I followed her back home,' Regan said.

'I've been checking on her, but she's never in. I considered speaking to her Highlander friends,' Leon said.

'What?' Regan growled.

'I wondered why she'd been so dismissive of you at the gig,' Leon said.

'Highlanders? Are you certain? How do you know?' Regan asked.

His eyes darted back and forth in shock.

'I know most things about Layla, including things she has yet to learn. If the Highlanders are going to act, and they may well do, we need to remain even more inconspicuous than we have to date.'

'What are you talking about?'

'She's rather unique, Regan! Layla ... I mean. She's very different to us. She was never changed by a vampire. It courses her veins and has done since birth. You know she still has a heartbeat. I know her father. My sister is *his* vamp!'

'Where is she?'

'South Africa,' Leon answered.

'What? When did she go there?' Regan asked, completely baffled.

'In 1907 when her vampire released her,' Leon answered.

'What are you talking about? Is Layla a century old?' Regan snarled.

'Oh! Um ... no; my sister is. Actually, she's more than a century and a half old now.'

Regan was shaking his head, totally bemused.

'Does she know about Layla?'

'No. My sister is a vindictive vamp, like most of them; consumed by blood and desire. Layla would be a threat to her,' he said.

'Why?' Regan asked.

'Connor let Marie go because Amara would have harmed her, but if she'd known about a child it could have been detrimental to all of them. He asked me to keep Marie safe and I've been watching Layla since the day she was born. At first I questioned her legitimacy, but Marie never replaced

Connor, or even attempted to. It was a very sad state of affairs for her. Layla has only been discovering the enormity of what she is since she lost her mother. I just keep my distance and make sure she's OK. Although she does have other protectors and the Highlanders, too, are a perfect deterrent,' Leon added.

Regan listened.

'I had no idea you were a vampire!' Leon stated.

'I wasn't at first,' Regan said.

'It just gets more and more complicated!' Leon said sardonically.

'How did you become immortal?' Regan asked.

Leon explained to Regan how his half-sister created his change. He told him about how she had done it to save him from death. At the time they had had no idea what the fatal disease killing him was, but it had grown worse as the years passed. He used to laugh when they said it had come from monkeys; he knew where it had come from and it certainly wasn't a monkey, long before 1981. His sister changed him after she arrived in South Africa from Belgium. She was his father's first child by a woman he met in the Belgian Congo. The woman was the daughter of a Belgian diplomat and her family would not allow his father to marry her because of his colour. She went back to Belgium where Amara was born as a human baby. She'd met her vampire at university, most unusual for a woman in the nineteenth century but after her change she obtained her degree and a few extra to boot, with ease. Amara was his first vamp, but when he changed his second vamp he fell in love with her and gave Amara her freedom. She had returned to South Africa to find her father, *his* father. She changed him then.

Their father rejected her and she lost her temperate mind and killed him and the guilt consumed her and made her more volatile. When Briege sent Connor to her (as reprisal for her enslavement to Joubert) Amara's decadence increased

172

further until she finally lost control and became a true vamp. She tended to be more lenient on him, although he could never understand why; vamps didn't care for anyone other than themselves.

'Amara knew how Marie felt – a blind man could have seen it – and she intended to kill her but Connor obstructed her. He has that gift but when he could not restrain Marie's thoughts he knew Amara would end Marie's life. He told Marie he wanted Amara because he felt bound to her. She had no idea what he was, or what bound actually meant, so she left. She was heartbroken and I did not enjoy watching her suffering. Connor knew she carried his child,' he said.

A bloody tear ran down Leon's face. Regan stared in disbelief as Leon wiped the blood away. He'd seen Layla's tears too.

'A release … picked up with age; not advisable in the public domain,' Leon said.

'Layla cries those tears too!'

'Odd,' Leon mused, 'she's very young. Must be her human emotions that aid the release; vampires generally don't feel such emotion in youth.'

'I know I don't have that ability but then I just assumed that was a male thing,' Regan said.

'Mmmm … Quite the contrary, it's the vamps who don't cry!'

'What now?' Regan asked.

'We observe. There are two of us now!'

'I could ask my friends to help,' he suggested.

'Too many vampires and that would only alert the Highlanders to our presence. It's probably best if we just keep it between us … for now,' Leon said.

Regan agreed, since it seemed Leon knew more about the Highlanders and Layla.

'When did you change, Regan? You and Layla met when you were human, right?'

Regan thought about his time at Glasgow University. He didn't want to reveal anything about Jimmy or his previous dysfunctional family. The most positive thing about his change had been his escape from them. He did sometimes think about paying his father a visit but he probably would have lost control.

'I was travelling through Europe. I stayed in Bruges for the summer,' Regan said.

'But there are no vampires in Belgium; not since Joubert anyway. The Vamp Council holds court there because there are no vampires in the city,' Leon said.

He gave a loud chuckle.

'I was human there,' Regan said.

Leon puzzled.

'I came to Glasgow University and went back to Ireland with two Irish friends. I don't remember much after that; they just disappeared. Next thing I knew I was in a nightmare. I can still feel the agony,' Regan said.

His eyes showed the pain of the venom entering his veins and his change. Leon remembered, even after such a long time, how excruciating it was; it was something that never left them.

'I ended up in a castle. The vamp and her coven were there,' Regan said.

'And you escaped ... obviously!'

'One of the vampires gave me a map and an address. I found the escapees in Aberdeen. I joined the band; Cara was in it too. Everything was fine until Cara was killed. That's why I've ended up back here again, trying to distract myself by haunting the casinos ...' Regan said.

For a moment they were silent, each in his own thoughts.

'She's quite spellbinding, isn't she?' Leon asked.

'Yeah,' Regan answered.

He was amazed how easily Leon could read his

174

expressions; he tried to keep his face straight. He didn't want Leon to recognise his lack of trust.

'We could take shifts … unless you have something better to do?' Leon suggested.

'How are you in daylight?' Regan asked.

'Fine. I'd say it's a little more difficult for you. You're still very young and you haven't found your shield yet. Mine is this band on my left wrist,' Leon said.

He showed Regan the band camouflaged by his ebony skin.

'It can be anything from your human life; you will have to try various objects with a hidden meaning for you. I assume you know why mine is so suitable. A word of warning: only expose the tip of your toe or the tip of your finger; it can be excruciating when you're testing for your shield,' Leon said.

He rolled up his sleeve to show Regan the scarring on his arm.

'Ooh!'

'It must be difficult for you to deny your craving. I'm a lot older than you and I still find it hard. I find the hospital blood banks most useful,' Leon said.

'Yeah, but I haven't succumbed to the human bouquet yet,' Regan said.

It fascinated Leon that such a young vampire could be so composed, although he did know one reason why that might have been so.

'I can see that. You're very pale. I've no doubt you tire easily, especially in daylight,' Leon said.

He recognised the signs.

'Regan, those who drink mortal blood from live humans are very powerful and not as pasty as you and I,' Leon said.

They laughed.

'I mean, I'm pasty to me,' he said.

'Do you have a coven?' Regan asked.

'No, I'm a loner. Getting away from my sister always keeps me on guard. Besides I'm gay!'

Regan choked and Leon laughed.

'You're safe,' he said.

'I've found a new love in my life: Raj, my polar opposite,' Leon said.

Regan tried to conceal his amusement at this camp vampire. 'I had no idea,' he fibbed.

'That I didn't fancy you?' Leon laughed. 'Or that vampires can be gay?'

Regan looked puzzled.

'I was always gay,' Leon went on. 'It followed me into this existence, much to Amara's disgust,' he said.

Regan nodded. He wasn't particularly surprised by Leon's remarks: being a vampire, after all, was more far-fetched than being gay. It was the twenty-first century, after all, but he wondered how Leon had fared a century ago ...

Leon interrupted his thoughts. 'Hey, don't worry about me. I coped!'

How did he know so many of my thoughts? Regan questioned silently.

Leon caught that one too. 'Many of us, in time, develop powers beyond the human. You already know about speed, agility and grace, but some have powers of the mind. I can see thoughts, for instance, but not thoughts a will chooses to suppress. I often had no idea what Layla was thinking; she's very deep. Most humans are really quite shallow,' he said.

'I must be a shallow vampire then!'

Leon laughed.

'I can't see them all. Only the ones you are so expressive with. You can't be a very good Poker player,' Leon laughed.

Regan laughed too.

'No, but I'm pretty great at blackjack,' he said.

'Ugh, no way ... you cheat. Counting cards isn't playing properly,' Leon laughed.

'I think you'll find it's more intelligent to count cards,' Regan chuckled.

'Anyway, with regard to Layla, I'll take the morning shift. I have to work tomorrow night,' Leon said.

Regan nodded and then, in one fluid movement, he turned and darted out the door.

'Mmmmm,' Leon sighed, as he remembered the young vampire's hard physique as the door swung to and fro after his departure.

I can hear you! Regan thought.

In his mind he heard Leon laughing uproariously.

Regan crouched opposite Layla's expensive, stylish home. He passed the time thinking of the scenarios that could have created such wealth. A tidy inheritance, a lucky investment, or perhaps a lucrative gambling habit (he thought of his own flutters). He wondered if all vampires obtained wealth by similar means or if some were more modest; the band had never seemed that short of money either. Did all vampires cheat using the 'gifts' Leon spoke of in this way? He wondered if others chose more ethical ways; like a career.

Suddenly Regan caught sight of Layla inside the house, looking out of her window, and once again she stunned him. Again, he could not imagine her as a hunter. She looked too perfect to have such animal instincts. But she had the ability, and he could understand her need for fresh blood; it was as natural as his. Suddenly the image of her stalking game enthralled him but the sound of her faint heartbeat threw him off course. He realised it was merely confirmation of what Leon said; human blood coursed through her veins. He could *hear* the evidence.

The allure of the scent forced him to struggle with mixed emotions, with guilt and desire. He had craved Cara's blood every time she had drawn near and at that moment he resented the burning sensation in his throat. Although he had never felt the deep yearning inside as he did when he saw Layla. He could see her so much clearer than before.

177

She was illuminated as she stared out from the window, into the night sky.

She caught sight of him. He flinched as her heartbeat accelerated and their eyes met; she did not let her gaze waver.

The window was open; he'd only caught a glimpse of her movement; she'd moved with such grace. He hesitated, then suddenly he was sitting on the sill and their gaze never faltered. He could feel her sweet, warm, breath on his face.

'I had no idea,' she fluted.

'I was human then,' he said.

'What happened to you?'

Layla's voice mesmerised him. She sang like a melody.

'It's a long story!'

Her cherry lips creased.

'Layla,' he said.

She placed her long, slender finger over his open mouth and pressed his lips together.

'I did not harm your friend,' she said.

Then she lowered her finger and her eyes glazed over.

'But I know who did,' she added.

She quivered, but it was not visible. She crossed her arms to cradle her inner motion.

'Layla,' he whispered, 'it wasn't Leon!'

He wanted to comfort her; he sensed her unease. He could do nothing until she invited him in.

'How do you know Leon?' she said.

She puckered her brow with a deep frown, expressing her confusion.

'Shush,' he said.

He looked over his shoulder and she watched, bemused, wondering what he was shushing her for. He was the one hovering on her window ledge. She humoured him anyway, although she knew her aunt would hear what she wanted of the conversation anyway. She decided not to cause him any more alarm so she didn't mention her; he already seemed a little anxious.

'Do you know what Leon is?' she whispered.

'Yes. It's pretty obvious,' he said.

She frowned, somewhat annoyed with his sarcasm.

'Gay,' Regan said.

'That's not funny,' she said.

'Oh go on … it is really. I do know he's a vampire though,' he said.

She was actually annoyed with herself. After all she hadn't noticed Leon was a vampire until after Cara's demise.

'I met him this evening at the restaurant; I was really waiting for you,' Regan explained.

'I asked him when you'd be working again. I needed to find out why you ran that night.'

'Why would you even believe him?'

'He is stronger, older, but definitely not wiser,' he chuckled.

'This is no laughing matter,' she scolded, 'we could all be put in danger!'

'He was trying to save her but he was too late … and … I *am* fully aware of the danger!'

He'd barely finished speaking when, in one rapid movement, she grabbed his hand, flew from the window, and they landed together on the path below, still hand in hand. She intended the rest of the conversation to be confidential. He stared, in awe of her. He'd not imagined such strength, power or grit and determination. For a moment they might have looked like young lovers walking in the moonlight. Layla suddenly dropped his hand.

Kate watched on and congratulated herself; her plan was beginning to run smoother than she had even anticipated. He seemed to be taking Layla's bait; she just needed to encourage her to reel him in.

A bit of gentle persuasion will help, she thought.

Regan placed Layla's hand back in his and took charge. He liked the intensity of the situation. She shook her hand free again. She didn't like to be dominated. She looked at him; his eyes were deeper and brighter than before, like sapphires in the dark, but with the same warmth. An electric current shot through her and she replaced her hand in his. He did not react, they fitted.

'Who was it then?' she whispered.

'I don't know, Layla. Cara had already been bled dry when Leon arrived. Her heart was not strong enough to absorb his venom. He knew you suspected him and he sensed us coming; he left to stop you getting hurt,' he said.

He wanted to tell her more of what Leon said, but it was not his tale to tell.

Regan's mind flitted with emotion – from lust to passion to guilt. His hand tightened around Layla's. Her heartbeat felt hypnotic.

At the edges of the city they began to run, flashing through the sky like twin comets. There was no moon and only one or two stars; they could see better in the dark. Below them they saw the dark glass of Loch Lomond and darted down to its shores, weaving in and out of the trees.

Suddenly he stopped and put his hand around her waist and pulled her to a stop beside him. He swung her to round face him. He tried to keep his movements slow, not wanting to startle her. He could hear her heartbeat fluttering and then leap as she pulled her frame forcefully to him. The vamp in her emerged. At first he was startled but when she placed her lips to his he forgot. At first he thought he would be drawn to her blood but her vampish ways seemed to quell his thirst. She moulded herself to him and he could feel how much warmer and softer she was in comparison to his cool, granite frame. He held her firm as they spiralled into a fantastical whirlwind ...

At last he pulled her away as gently as he could.

180

'You're quite demanding,' he laughed, 'and yet you're the picture of innocence.'

'It's the vamp in me,' she giggled.

He took her hand. The sky had started to take on the tints of dawn and they knew they must put their attraction aside for a while. The electricity they created was intense. To control their emotions was as complex as abstaining from the mortal drink.

As they reached her front door and he turned to leave, the sun was not far off the horizon and he felt drained. The amulet glistening in his sapphire eyes as he gazed into her emerald eyes and bid her goodnight.

'Will you be back later?' she said.

'That's the plan. Leon will be here too,' he called.

'I don't need protecting, Regan!'

'Ooh. You can be temperamental,' he teased.

'Stop mocking me. You know how changeable we are,' she grumbled.

'OK. Imagine we're protecting our identity, not you,' he said.

She calmed down and he kissed her gently, then turned and fled.

'I hear you have quite a few protectors anyway,' he shouted back.

'What's that supposed to mean?' she fumed loudly. She knew he could hear, but he did not answer.

'I know exactly what you mean!'

She went into the house.

'Oh, Aunt Kate!' she paused. 'I wasn't expecting you there,' she said.

'So I see.' Kate's tone was a little odd. 'Where were you?' Kate struggled to contain her annoyance. She needed Layla on side if she didn't want to destroy her plan.

'Oh, just out for a walk,' Layla said.

'Strange time to go for a walk.'

'There are fewer people around,' Layla fibbed.

'Yes well, maybe you could let me know next time,' Kate snarled.

'Right, yeah. What's with the overprotective tone?' Layla retorted. 'I usually hunt at night after all,' she added.

Kate changed the subject. 'Do you want a coffee?'

'No, I'm working later. I'll lie down!'

'I thought you'd left,' Kate said.

'I need the money,' she said.

'No you don't!'

'Yes I do. I like paying my own way,' she insisted.

'OK. No need to be so stubborn,' Kate said.

'No need to be so quick tempered,' Layla flung back as she flew upstairs to her room.

Kate dashed out the door, eager to regain her equilibrium. Retribution was her ultimate goal and Layla was playing the lead role in her little pantomime. She couldn't let her temper stand in the way of that. She intended to wreak havoc but not yet.

Colleen would be the first to suffer. This vampire of Layla's would lure the Irish vamp straight into her trap.

He would definitely be invited in.

18

The Gathering

Frazer summoned Duncan and Ewan to a gathering at the Stone of Destiny. Duncan was still in turmoil about what he should do about Layla. He doubted, given the bloody events in Glasgow, that either Ewan or Uncle Frazer would share his views. In fact, he was certain they would insist the matter be taken in hand.

They left at dawn, driving silently. Duncan was trying to hide his discomposure. He avoided conversation to ensure they didn't discuss Layla. He was desperately trying to find a solution that would protect Layla, knowing she posed no threat to them or those they had vowed to protect.

They parked the car at the foot of the brae. It was a bright day but they had a long hike through the remote landscape and the light would fade fast. They trekked along unmarked paths, pushing back wild plants and flowers, thistles and brambles as they passed. They covered countless miles of braes and valleys to the secret meeting point. The real Stone, of course, had never gone to England; no Scot would ever countenance that. Only three knew, though, of its true resting place and its true meaning. It was the entrance to the tomb of their ancestors, a mere myth to their country's inhabitants but a reality for the Highlanders. They had enemies and so did their people – some in the mortal world and some in the immortal.

They sat among the heather on the banks of a burn and ate their lunch in silence, both deep in thought. It was a momentous occasion, the second time they were gathering at the Stone, their ancestral burial ground. Uncle Frazer was the only Highlander of the three who had connected with the other realm before. Being a Highlander was a great honour and to protect your people was a dream for those who loved their country to the core.

Frazer stood atop the brae looking over the horizon and their approach. He gestured a greeting with his hefty sword as it glinted in the final rays of the sun. Ewan, with Duncan still a few paces behind, climbed the ancient burial mound. They wore the traditional Highland dress, the kilts of their kith and kin, and their sporrans and swords were adorned with the heraldic crest of a lone piper. The swords they carried were polished and sharpened with precision. As Duncan took his final step onto the summit of the brae, they greeted one another.

Frazer lit the fire he had prepared as he waited. He threw a log onto the dry grass and moss and within a short time it roared, removing the chill from the atmosphere.

Frazer called the gathering to order as he poured and 'swalleed a wee dram oot tha cupp'o welcome'. He passed the Highland quaich to Ewan, who held its two handles and drank from the shallow bowl. He, in turn, passed the primitive, staved wooden bowl to Duncan, who drank the fine scotch. The meeting opened and they passed the relic around until it was dry. It had been given to Frazer by the previous key-holder of the Realm. Ewan cooked offal stew in an iron cauldron as Frazer refilled the quaich. They supped and drank while reminiscing about times past, and enjoyed the company of their alter-egos. They spoke of being trained in the way of the sword and their loyalty to their kinfolk. Frazer informed them of their need to uphold the traditions of their forefathers. Uncle Frazer prided himself on the outstanding abilities of his students who had proven to be worthy Protectors.

Duncan loved his country and his heritage but he also loved Layla. He had no idea how much, until he realised her identity and what this meant. He wondered if Frazer knew that she was still part human. Nonetheless he could not be certain if it would affect Uncle Frazer or save her from what he intended for her kind. He doubted, too, if Ewan's commitment to her was as steadfast as his commitment to the Realm. Highlanders were chosen because of their natural strength, ability and power as well as their inbred loyalty to protect their fellow countrymen. He puzzled over his dilemma all night as he watched Uncle Frazer and Ewan slowly fall into a drunken stupor under the starless sky. His mind felt anything but clear but his thoughts kept him sober and serious.

Dawn broke with a white mist in the air; dew lay on the blades of grass. Duncan stoked the embers of the fire and threw a log on to warm them. The sun always had little heat until it sat higher in the sky. He stood at the top of the hill watching the sun rising slowly lighting the sky and bringing the loch below them into view.

Ewan stretched as Duncan returned to the fire. He was punch-drunk and his mouth felt like a sewer. They all reeked of smoke and stale whisky. The only pleasant smell came from the heather on the ground and the thistles fixed to the sheepskins they had covered themselves with. Duncan's eyes were bulging from his sleepless night, imprinted with red webs of the alcohol that still coursed through his veins.

'Morning, Dunc,' Ewan teased.

Duncan nodded, forcing a smile.

'Morning, boys,' Uncle Frazer bellowed in his deep, grizzly voice.

He looked fresh as a daisy and, even though he had drunk plenty, he had slept deep, as evidenced by his snores. Duncan, as solemn as he felt, could not help but see the funny side.

'Your snores could wake the dead! I expect that's why you were given the Key to the Realm,' he chuckled.

Ewan rolled with laughter.

'I don't know what you're laughing at. You weren't far behind him,' Duncan added.

'Duncan, no harm, but you can raise the roof yourself,' Ewan laughed. 'It's obvious now. We were all chosen for our snoring abilities.'

They all laughed. Uncle Frazer's deep laughter echoed through the landscape.

After a plentiful breakfast of the previous night's leftovers, Uncle Frazer addressed them in Gaelic; the matters they needed to discuss were far more serious than those of the previous night. Duncan and Ewan spoke the Highlanders' mother tongue fluently, although they routinely spoke English to keep their identities secret.

'Have you decided what to do about the vampires?' Frazer asked.

Ewan nodded forcefully but Duncan's head remained static. Frazer noted their responses. 'I myself believe we should act before there is any further carnage. We can remove the instigators ourselves and thereby avoid having to reopen the tomb of the other Highlanders. As you both know we must all be in agreement.'

Uncle Frazer watched them closely. Ewan's decision was predictable but Duncan was hesitant.

Ewan spoke first, just as Frazer had surmised.

'I agree. I think we should dispose of them before the problem escalates. The flat below mine in Aberdeen is definitely a haven for at least three of them,' he revealed. 'We can start there.'

Duncan felt a wave of relief. Ewan's disclosure had given him an unexpected diversion.

'I agree,' he spurted.

Uncle Frazer remained silent. He was surprised; he

thought Duncan would have taken more persuading, which made his hasty reply dubious. The purge was necessary and the vamp who had come to Burns Night ceilidh would be dealt with in due course. A vote confirmed all in favour for them to start at Ewan's flat. The date of the first removal had been agreed.

Uncle Frazer refilled the quaich, and they passed it around to mark their farewells. They kissed the Stone of Destiny and the gathering closed.

Duncan arrived at Ewan's flat before Uncle Frazer. They discussed the tactics Uncle Frazer had instructed them to use. The vampires had to be beheaded, burned and scattered on foreign soil. This ensured that the body would not reform and that they were removed from Scotland permanently. Ewan was fixated with staking the vampires in their coffins and Duncan stared at him in disbelief. He was pretty sure Ewan had been reading too many horror stories; they weren't dealing with Count Dracula, after all. Anyway, he was fairly confident they weren't sleeping in coffins, wearing long black capes and slicking back their hair.

Duncan felt strangely guilty about agreeing to execute them so cruelly. After all, they were hiding their identities (just as the Highlanders did) and from what he could tell they even steered clear of human blood. Duncan believed the campfires, good and bad, were all being tarred with the same brush. He would have to tell Ewan about Layla. He didn't relish it, but he knew he had to do it before Uncle Frazer did. He guessed the ghillie's story would have sounded far more sinister than the truth.

When at first he broached the subject, Ewan laughed, but he soon realised Duncan was being deadly serious. He was flabbergasted, rendered speechless, and Duncan reminded him how fond they both were of Layla and that had he not told him about her, he may never have known. In fact, Ewan now knew and suddenly his loyalties felt divided. He became annoyed with Duncan, he wished he could rewind the previous few minutes, because Layla's identity changed everything so dramatically. She could not exist in their world, or be part of it, history and heritage dictated that, and he wondered how Duncan could tell him something so dramatic in such a calm manner. He couldn't get his head around her fantastical form.

'How long have you known about her?'

'Since the Burns Night celebrations,' Duncan confirmed.

'So you've had all this time to process what she is. Why didn't you tell me sooner?'

'I didn't know how you would take the information. You hate them so much and I was wary about how you would react.'

'You've chosen a hell of time to tell me.'

'I had to tell you before Uncle Frazer did.'

'He knows too?' Ewan shouted.

'Shush … the vampires above us will hear you. Yes, he knew from the minute he laid eyes on her.'

Ewan puzzled for a moment. He sensed Frazer watching Layla but he never, for one minute, ever thought it because she could be a vampire. He couldn't even imagine Layla being the callous, cruel being Frazer and history described her as but that was exactly what she was.

'How?'

'She was born to a vampire.'

'And where's he?'

'She doesn't know him. He doesn't seem to be in Scotland.'

'What cloud are you living in Duncan? You had no idea there were vampires living in Aberdeen and right under our noses so to speak.'

'True,' he couldn't argue with Ewan, he was right but then Ewan had no inclination of Layla, however her human side hid the more alarming part of her.

'Regardless of what I think Uncle Frazer will surely want Layla destroyed.'

'And could you be the one to do that?'

'If I have to … yes.'

'Just as I suspected; she's part human and that makes at least half of her worth protecting. We could stand together and tell Uncle Frazer we don't want him to harm her.'

'I can't agree to that!'

Duncan nodded. He'd heard there was a very fine line between love and hate and it seemed Ewan was proof of that.

'We've other vampires to worry about first and not much time in which to do it,' Ewan said.

'Aye …'

19

Proof of Virtue

Regan met Layla after her shift, after dark. They walked at a steady pace, mimicking the stride of humans. It was always harder when walking with another vampire and, because they made such a terribly handsome couple, people were automatically drawn to their presence. Thankfully that was all – mortal vision was too limited to penetrate deeper, to see their hidden torment.

Layla seemed so much calmer than he, although he did know that there were times when her thoughts were as dark as his. They, however, were their own distraction; their emotional bond meant they could distract themselves with one another. They talked of his life in Aberdeen, his touring with the band and their gigs, as normal things as possible, and their conversations were intense and enthusiastic. They forgot themselves in each other.

As they walked up the hill in the direction of Layla's house, he felt the muted beating in her chest begin to quicken. Regan's physical presence corrupted her dignity; the flutters, she could feel, were proof. The attraction was mutual, which made it even more powerful. As they reached the front door of her house he kissed her before his brain ignited. He thought of the irony of it all – how he'd been almost shackled to the last vamp and escaped her control, and yet now he wanted nothing more than to be under Layla's control for that moment. He tried to mask the sensations of his aching groin as he tormented remembering how similar the sensations had felt that night Colleen changed him. He suppressed all such thoughts as he kissed Layla, tentatively at first but then with growing intensity. In the blink of an eye the kiss became powerful as they hungered more and more for one another, but then suddenly he flinched and pulled back.

In an instant, with no verbal communication, they drew apart sharply. He dashed from the step and she through the front door. The electricity had shocked them both.

Layla lay on her bed and imagined running her hands through his dark hair, entangling her fingers in his locks as she pulled him to her. She'd memorised the touch of his lips and relived the passion in daydream. Her heart quickened and a shiver ran up her spine. She quivered visibly.

Regan smelled her scent lingering on him; the ache did not ease. For once the pain was not his throat; it was far more intense. She was nothing like Colleen in form or presence. He could see her in his thoughts; he could feel her presence still.

Layla had the night off so her aunt conveniently made plans to be out. His return was essential. She suspected Layla would not invite him in while she was there so her plan would ensure things moved forward in her favour.

Regan arrived and the door opened before he even knocked. She stood, majestic before him; her intoxicating scent drowned his senses.

'Please come in,' she stated.

She smiled. Her eyes shone with excitement and apprehension; she was visibly shaking.

He didn't know what to do. He hesitated, surprised by her sudden invitation. He could walk over the threshold at any point.

'Are you coming in or not?' she asked.

He took an uneasy step as she raised her eyes to meet his. She stared longingly into his sapphire eyes and he knew at that moment that she had extended more than a mere invitation to enter the house. She could tell the feelings were mutual; his pupils had dilated to almost cover his crystal gaze. Regan's groin ached and he stepped over the threshold to the faint, but fast, beating in her chest.

'Can I get you anything?' she asked. Only a polite turn of phrase; she didn't expect he wanted anything ... other than her blood.

He smiled, sensing the tiny flutter in the rhythm of her heartbeat. The smile reminded her of her intentions and she grabbed his hand. She pulled him behind her, but instinct held him firmly to the spot. He was strong but she was stronger. He saw his feet lift from the ground as her force dragged him for a split second and then he kept pace.

'Layla?'

He stopped. She stood a stair above him; he could feel her breath on his face. She did not loosen her firm hold on his hand; instead she shushed him by kissing him. Her energy compelled him and, even after she had let go of his hand, he followed her wilfully and will-lessly, captivated by her spirited actions as finally his actions mirrored hers.

Candlelight filled her bedroom. He started as she blew an explosive gust to extinguish the flames.

She sauntered, as best a vamp could, over to him and, suddenly, seducing him became a very natural instinct to her. The vamp had finally emerged. She ripped off her blouse, and, although he wanted to object, he remained entranced. He'd caught sight of her pert breasts below the light material. He disregarded his good intentions and pulled her to him firmly. They ran their faces over one another trying to hold back their need to consume one another. A split second later, Layla had torn off his clothes. Wanton and determined she lost her composure. They met skin to skin for the first time, he cool against her warmer exterior. He rippled like stone against her soft, but durable, form.

He brushed his fingers over her full lips and placed one hand on the small of her back, pulling her tighter to him. She groaned but not in pain. Their lips parted, tasting the difference of one another. They did not love as humans – they loved faster and stronger – but there were a few similarities, namely the more emotion involved the deeper the intensity of the physical love.

Layla wrapped herself around him and they lay back as he enfolded her in his arms.

They never tired. Another bonus for vampires, it meant their love making was as endless as they were. They repeated the crescendo; their minds grew with each intricate detail of the moment. They had plenty of room and never-ending spaces to fill.

The front door slammed and they looked at one another. It wasn't as endless as they had anticipated. Aunt Kate never slammed the door and it was odd that she should. Layla jumped up as they both embraced and speedily dressed. Regan soared from the window; he blew her a kiss and landed on the footpath below.

Duncan stood at the foot of the stairs.

20

Return of the Vamp

She stood head in hands, cursing her foolishness. Sentiment was forbidden and yet she'd allowed it to rule her thoughts. Desire encompassed her existence and the role of seductress fitted her persona, but Colleen enjoyed giving pleasure too, although this was out of character for a vamp. She didn't enjoy executions; they were a necessary evil to keep her true self hidden from her sister's suspicious mind. Ignoring the soothing attentions of Daniel, Colleen's thoughts wandered to Briege and to the atrocities of which she was capable.

Briege dictated and controlled all vamps and their covens equally. She was the strongest and oldest vamp, though she was also the most victimised. One of her vampires did escape her; he cleverly concealed himself in human society in Scotland. The Highlanders would never have suspected what he was, and since he knew Briege would never have broken her agreement with the Highlanders he lived there unexposed for many years. Briege, however, never forgot. She eventually used her cunning and ventured north of Cavan to the Antrim coast of Ireland, a long time before Colleen even developed her coven. She found two young, local males; both 'off their faces' in drug-induced stupors, which made them easy to seduce. Plus they already had the pallid skin and dark eyes of a vampire so their appearance seemed unchanged when she did turn them. They took to vampirism with ease, hypnotised quickly into Briege's brutal existence. They were happy to live under her control because their new-found addiction didn't come with the same expensive price tag. Their new drug of pleasure was readily available and Briege did not deny them the right to obtain it, although the substance was just as illegal as any of the street drugs they purchased as humans. Her only stipulation was that they hide their true identity when satisfying their craving for the mortal essence.

Briege kept the hunting habits of her new vampires hidden. She sweetened her taking of them by offering them as hunters to the Council's covens. The hunters could find and entice suitable males to a region for a vamp seeking a new mate. Kite and Franky tracked escapees and hunted for victims. They became her eyes and ears in Scotland with John's retrieval as their priority. Her foremost idea was to restore her pride and that could only be achieved when her escapee met his doom.

Briege was Head Vamp on the Council. Another vamp would have been severely punished if a vampire had escaped; she reiterated this to her vamps incessantly. Many were punished for far lesser crimes. However, since she enforced the rules, no vamp dared question her.

Franky and Kite enjoyed the fervour of the chase. Franky, in particular, relished the gore; the end result being mortal essence and the ultimate high. Tracking was like a sport to him. He believed their victims were being freed into immortality. He enjoyed his existence and did not live in torment.

'We found him,' Franky smirked.

Briege glared. Then her lips turned upwards, a most unusual shape for her mouth. She flashed her white teeth and the reflection of light blinded Franky for an instant, making him blink.

'John,' Kite said.

He paused, unsure how Briege would receive the other information they had learned.

Briege glared at him, warning him to divulge all they knew. He cleared his throat.

'He's married,' Franky spouted.

His words would not have been coherent to human ears. He'd spoken so quickly it would have been perceived as a mumble by mortals. He lowered his eyes, not wanting to see the reaction on her face.

'What do you mean?' Briege snarled.

Kite backed away but Franky stood firm; he'd not seen the scowl she'd given Kite. They stood taller than her small frame, but she dwarfed them with her power. She chose, however, to conceal her anger; the messengers would not be executed for a time.

'Go on!' she insisted.

'He married a human woman. She's definitely Irish, although she has lived in Glasgow a long time and developed a Glaswegian twang. She definitely has an Irish tone to her voice,' Franky said.

He normally spoke with a strong voice, and, of the two vampires, he was the more confident. Kite regularly referred to him as 'cocksure' of himself. Now his voice quivered.

'She's human?' she almost shouted. Her eyes darkened. She was seething and hissing with disapproval. She could hear her voice still echoing; it was then she lowered her tone and unclenched her fangs.

'You're sure?'

She was glaring at Franky.

'Yes ... she was very tempting!'

'What Franky means is,' Kite interrupted, 'it confirmed her humanity.'

'Just as well you didn't do anything stupid then. It could have been very costly to you both,' she scowled.

They took a further step back.

'Well done for using your initiative,' she said.

Again, she held back the instinct within her to punish them. They nodded at her approval, never sure of the true meaning of her words. Alarm bells rang in Briege's ears. She considered allowing the vampires to execute the wife, but she wouldn't allow her suffering to end so prematurely. Existing in hell and remembering his torture for eternity; that would be punishment far more fitting for her, more than mere death. She smiled, pleased with her ingenious idea, engulfed in her own lunacy.

She gave Franky and Kite a different assignment. If they followed her orders and returned with no problems she would consider them worthy subjects and perhaps spare them the agonies she had already planned for them.

They carried out her orders and lured John and his wife back into Briege's grasp. John soon discovered where his fate lay. Briege, moreover, recognised his wife, which only fuelled her fury the more. He had chosen his wife over her ... a local girl! It confirmed to Briege that she must have known what he was and that he belonged to her, and that sealed her fate.

'Please, Briege,' John begged, 'take me but let her go. She has a sister.'

His begging only made her angrier; the emotion in his voice showed how deeply he felt for his wife. Briege viewed any feelings with contempt.

'It was me ... it was my idea ... mine alone,' he lied.

Briege knew he was lying. *He* would never have chosen to endanger her.

'I won't end her life,' Briege said. Her tone was low and even. 'I will preserve it,' she smirked.

'Please, don't!' he begged.

His voice trailed off into the distance as they carried him to the entrance. His protestations were futile. His distress was obvious by the pain on his face as he stood in the tunnel of trees.

They all watched. The vamps, vampires, his wife and his best friend all suffered his demise. Colleen watched but she could not bring herself to take part and Briege joined three other vamps for their merciless act of torture.

Colleen wondered at what point Briege had become so brutally cruel. Had it been before or after Myntie's demise? Myntie had uprooted her from her family as a young seventeen-year-old girl and enticed her with prospects of marriage. She moved to Scotland with him where she soon discovered what he had planned for her. Briege loved him and embraced their life together. It pleased her that death would never part them.

Briege was gentle and kind even after Myntie changed Colleen as soon as she was old enough. Briege remained true; she was head of his household and Colleen their child. It wasn't until he took more vamps that Briege protested. The vamps were for his simple pleasure and Briege was often the victim of his wrath. When Myntie turned his attentions to Colleen it turned Briege. That was the ultimate act of betrayal. From that moment on, it seemed, she lived in torment until the Highlanders killed him and freed her. But with that she lost her willpower too. She had been intent on revenge and her soul solidified into stone. She herself had tried to follow Briege's example, but there was something missing; not enough self-hate, she supposed.

Colleen was surprised to be interrupted by Franky and Kite since she had not summoned them and she had no intention of extending her coven.

'Hi Colleen,' Franky said.

Daniel got up and left the room. It was unimaginable that a vampire's face could have been any paler, or maybe it was the darkening of his eyes that made it seem so. He didn't excuse himself; he just made a dash for the exit.

'Hi,' Colleen said.

She watched Daniel leave and felt slightly discontented.

'What are you two doing here?'

'Just a flying visit,' Kite sniggered.

Franky choked with laughter.

Colleen watched them, not amused. She found the two vampires a bit painful. They consistently cracked stupid jokes and never got to the point. She wasn't really in the mood.

'Get to the point. You obviously have a reason for being here,' she said.

'All right, keep your knickers on,' Kite chuckled.

Colleen crouched and growled. She meant business; they were really beginning to irritate her.

'OK, sorry. It's the Yank; we've found him,' Kite said.

'What?'

'The Yank! Kite and I found him,' Franky said.

'The American, but where?' she said, shocked.

'Glasgow,' Franky added.

'Scotland!' she said.

'Aye, that's where Glasgow is!'

She growled. Franky was an obnoxious, sarcastic piece of work; she didn't like him at all. In fact, she could barely stomach either him or Kite. She would gladly have erased them had she been given the opportunity, but Briege seemed to rate them highly, so she avoided confrontation. She often wished she'd never even entertained the American; it had been a nightmare.

'Franky, give it a rest. The girl's obviously surprised,' Kite warned. They'd annoyed enough; they didn't need to push it too far. He knew she could turn on them and, although she was not much of a problem for them, her vampires outnumbered them.

'How did you find him?' Colleen went on.

'We weren't really looking. He just happened to be in the

area at the same time we were. He sings and he's got a girl,' Kite said.

'He sings,' she said.

'Aye, pretty well, actually,' Kite added. Franky was singing a tune in the background.

'Shut up!' she said.

She glared at him. He gave a final hum, and then clasped his jaws. Kite was glaring at him too.

'I can't go to Scotland. It's forbidden,' she said.

'So is letting a vampire escape!' Franky was sniggering and sneering. As much as she wanted to growl the vampire did have a point; but, more than that, she couldn't trust these two nuisances not to tell Briege. They obviously knew too much and she had no choice but to attempt to retrieve the American or destroy him. If she didn't her coven would most definitely suffer.

'Oh and something else that might help you...' Franky said. Then he paused and waited for a more grateful response.

She glared at him but he did not flinch. He just added in a matter-of-fact manner, 'The Yank has a brother.'

Colleen waited, wondering what the relevance of the statement was.

'And?' she returned impatiently.

'And,' Franky said, mocking her word and tone of voice, 'he's one of your fellow housemates.'

Instantly Colleen lunged at him. She grabbed him by the throat and growled into his face. He did not flinch. He just looked at her in amusement. She had more to lose than him.

When her coven appeared at the door Franky winced slightly and he broke free from her grasp and he and Kite fled. Franky was shouting back at her as he flew through the air, as ever having the last word, 'You should probably do something before we do!' and his cold laugh echoed from the hilltops and through the rooms of the castle.

The vampires stood sheepishly, their gaze fixed on the floor, knowing she had discovered what they'd done.

'Which one of you is it?' she bellowed.

'Me,' Daniel said.

'No,' Jimmy said, 'you're not taking the rap for me.'

'Jimmy,' Daniel said, 'I planned it. I used you. I didn't want Regan to stay. I was afraid Colleen might dismiss me.'

Colleen growled. She crouched.

'You've destroyed us all! I have to destroy him or Briege will execute all of us,' she shouted.

'No, not if we get him back,' Daniel said.

'I don't want him back. I don't want him to have this existence,' Jimmy said.

Colleen lunged at Jimmy.

'I'll send you to the Council,' she said.

'Please do,' he whispered and stood firm.

'That's a good idea,' Daniel said, 'if Regan thinks Jimmy has been sent to the Council he would come back.'

'No!'

'You don't have a choice,' Daniel shouted. He lunged at Jimmy but Padar intervened.

'No, I'm with Jimmy,' he said, 'I know you love Colleen but that's your choice. We don't have one.'

Colleen looked at Daniel as he turned to her.

'It was me who found you, Colleen. I know you think you discovered me but I knew what you were and I wanted to be with you. I wanted you to change me so we could be together for ever,' Daniel said.

'Well, bigger fool you. You don't choose this; you are chosen,' she said. 'I'm going to Glasgow!'

'Please, Colleen ... don't! ... It's not safe,' Daniel begged.

'If you love me, as you say you do, then you will make sure the rest of the vampires do not try to stop me,' she shouted.

She flew out the door. Jimmy and Padar tried to pull her back as she had anticipated but Daniel threw himself at them. They battered one another like crashing rocks until Colleen had disappeared from view. They were two against his one but Daniel seemed to have more strength than ever before, as though unveiling his secret had empowered him. He fought them off and disabled them. He eventually released them when he knew she must be far enough away.

'If you follow her, you may reveal your brother's existence. Colleen will only want him to return with her. If they haven't returned by sundown we'll pursue her … for both their sakes. Agreed?' Daniel asked.

'Agreed!'

21

Protection

Leon was on watchman duties. It was almost dawn when two animated lads walked toward him along the pavement. They seemed to be heading home after a night on the tiles. Anyone could have been mistaken for thinking they were two merry men but Leon recognised them instantly. He'd followed them once before when they'd shadowed Layla. They could have spent day and night on the town and were an all too familiar sight in Glasgow of late. They didn't seem perturbed that the sun was on the horizon, but then Leon knew all too well what finding a protective symbol meant to a vampire. These two were not afraid of showcasing their identities or that the Highlanders had become suspicious of vampire presence.

Leon gawped as they turned and walked straight up to Kate's front door. The back of one of them was etched in his mind. He remembered all too well the night Cara had become his victim. The red-haired vampire hadn't been there that night; it was the raven-haired vampire who had been Cara's attacker. He watched, wary. Fight or flight? He was certain he had years on the vampires, but he had not fed for a while and felt too malnourished to overpower them.

Leon shook his head to dissolve his distracting thoughts and returned his attentions to Layla. He could see her shadow through the blinds; he regularly glimpsed her this way at dawn; she seemed to sleep very little. He used all the strength he could muster to enter Layla's thoughts. He had never been successful before, but it was imperative that he warn her about the two vampires standing on her threshold. He was too late. He heard the knock and Layla dashing down the stairs. He gasped as she opened the door to them. She did not invite them in, but even before she could speak they had crossed the threshold without hesitation.

Layla caught sight of Leon before she closed the door and instantly acknowledged the message he was sending her. She knew not to give anything away.

Clever girl, Leon thought.

He saw her close the door and call her aunt. She excused herself before her aunt entered the room and, before he could blink, she was crouched beside him. He signalled her not to speak. He wanted to grab her and take her to safety but she was too independent for that; they needed to stay to find out what the two vampires wanted. It had been her aunt they asked for.

Inside the house Kate welcomed her guests.

'Where's Layla?' Kate said.

'She went to her room,' Kite answered.

'Just as well.' Franky added. 'It's probably a bit early to let her know what's about to unfold.'

He had a cruel tone to his voice. Kite looked at him; certain Franky was getting more wicked by the day. He didn't seem tormented at all, and the more Franky embraced their demonic deeds, the more tormented Kite felt. Kate shushed Franky. She was all too aware of how extreme Layla's abilities were.

'Layla!' Kate called.

Outside Layla looked at Leon. He put his hand on hers, firmly gesturing her not to move, and she remained silent.

'I thought as much,' Kate said. 'She usually leaves when I

have visitors. We have a mutual respect for one another's privacy,' she smirked.

Franky sniggered.

'She's on her way,' Kite said, 'just as you instructed.'

'Good,' Kate said.

Layla turned to Leon again; they were both baffled.

'Does she know where he is?' Kate asked.

'No. That's why we came here. She'll follow our scent,' Franky said.

There was a knock at the door and Kate invited Colleen in.

Leon and Layla had already left to warn Regan. This would most certainly spell trouble. Layla was in shock.

'Leon,' she cried.

He held her. He had anticipated something like this was in the pipeline. He knew it the day he had taken Marie from her coffin and brought her to his home. Kate had been draining the life from her for months; only when he visited did he notice how weak she was and how little time she had before dying. He'd gained entry into the house by posing as a doctor and had given her his blood in a transfusion. He did this a second time when Kate and Layla were out for a day trip, fed from her and bound her to him by giving her his blood again. Then he took her away, collecting her body in a hearse. Layla had a lot to take in; it wasn't the time to introduce her to Marie. Leon sensed Layla's emotions; he couldn't see her thoughts but he knew that her discovery of her aunt's true intentions and her deceitful ways would be distressing her. He'd never been certain of Kate's plan but at that moment it became crystal clear to him.

'She's brought Colleen here to take Regan!' Layla cried.

'No, she's lured Colleen here using Regan as bait, but Briege will be her main target. Colleen is guilty of letting her vampire escape from the coven and Briege will want them both punished,' Leon said. He didn't want to use the word *execute* and alarm her further.

205

'Why didn't you tell me?' she said.

'I wasn't certain until Colleen arrived. She had a very well-executed plan. Still she doesn't yet know that we've uncovered it, and Briege is not here yet. It's her we need to deter from coming,' Leon said.

'What about Regan?'

'We have to tell him,' Leon said. 'If the Highlanders discover Colleen is here there will be a lot of trouble. It could initiate a bitter battle. Briege cannot come here; it could be fatal for all of us because, if Briege comes here, the agreement is broken. Kate wants Briege here to initiate a war.'

'She wants to avenge Uncle John,' Layla said.

'Yes. That's the thing about us, Layla; retribution can become our whole existence unless we learn to deal with those bitter emotions. I've never seen such logic in another vampire other than Regan, you're part human which explains how even tempered you are generally, but his control is amazing.'

'I could tell Duncan,' she said.

'There have been enough fatalities already. Perhaps that would not be the best thing to do at this time. Regan will have to confront Colleen.'

'No!' she shouted.

'Layla, that is his decision, and he needs to make it if he wants to prevent fuelling a very bitter rivalry that time has not yet relieved,' he said.

Leon knew Regan would not want Layla to be in any danger. Briege had no idea Layla existed, and if she did she would have wanted her destroyed. Knowing Briege's history meant her stance was firmly 'No Vamps in Scotland Ever' and Layla, in maturity, would have more power than all the vamps put together; however, she was not fully mature and therefore still quite vulnerable. But at the moment...

Leon had to admire Kate. She was the one who had

instructed Kite and Franky to find someone for Colleen and had played everything and everyone perfectly ... except for him of course. She had no idea of his presence.

As much as he knew Layla would be heartbroken at losing Regan, he was not his concern. He had no allegiance to Regan and in Leon's mind he belonged to Colleen anyway, even though their 'relationship' had not yet been consummated. Regan was a vampire in his own right and capable of his own protection. Layla and Marie were his only concern.

22

Gone or Forgotten

Duncan was in the shower. The black liquid ran down his strong chest, body and legs and into the plughole. He washed his auburn hair to rid himself of the ash, the smell of fire and the reminder of what he and Ewan had just done. He felt merciless but he agreed to it to save Layla. He wondered how he would live with himself; it had felt almost savage. The vampires had not caused any unnecessary harm and in fact lived quietly in society for decades, even before he and Ewan were born. Duncan even remembered seeing the band in Glasgow, at Layla's eighteenth; he had no idea what they were although it seemed Ewan did. They had destroyed them just for being.

Ewan did not seem perturbed by any of it. It was his duty and it was not their choice to make. He realised he'd been infatuated by Layla's physical presence; in fact, he wondered how he could ever have been so entranced by her. He thought she must have hypnotised him. He shook his head to dispel the image. He'd agreed to spare her, but, if he was honest with himself, he wasn't so sure it was the best course of action. There were two more of them she had taken under her wing and they most certainly could not be saved. He and Duncan would have to address the matter soon.

They walked along the footpath, in their full attire, as

though they were going to a Highland games, caber tossing and the like. In fact, they had far more sinister plans for that night. As they went up to Layla's aunt's door Layla was walking toward them.

It was silent.

Duncan could not lift his head to meet her gaze. He felt disloyal to her; his loyalty to Scotland had taken precedence and yet she filled his whole being. Ewan kept his eyes firmly on her.

'Head up,' he said to Duncan.

Duncan glared at him. He'd taken Ewan at his word. Instinct took over and he ran to save her. But before he reached her she was flanked by the dark-skinned vampire and another figure. The missing member of the band; Ewan wondered where he was; he stopped questioning how he'd not recognised the chemistry between the vampire and Layla before.

'I told you,' he said, 'they can't be trusted.'

Kate was staring out the window. It couldn't have gone better for her. The scene outside was something she had envisaged so many times before. It seemed surreal. Colleen, Franky and Kite stood beside her, bemused. It was a worst-case scenario for them. They had drawn the attention of the Highlanders and for that reason Briege would surely intervene.

Layla found herself wishing there were some *real* humans around, but for some strange reason the streets were quiet with no one to be seen. As her mind spun she realised it not so strange: the Highlanders would obviously have kept any Scotsman from danger; they had planned everything meticulously.

'Can we talk?' Leon said.

Ewan was poised for attack. Duncan raised his hand to signal him to remain calm. Fury seemed to be running out of Ewan's every pore. Suddenly Frazer was beside them.

Duncan was surprised; he had not been expecting him. Ewan, however, did not flinch; he obviously knew he was coming. Behind Frazer, in the distance an omnipotent lone figure stood, watching. Layla looked around her wondering if any of the others could see him. She was distracted when Kate led the other vampires out. Leon's eyes darkened. With those four around the situation would surely have turned into something sinister. Frazer's smug demeanour did not ease his tension.

'I just want to go with my vamp,' Regan said. He had to defuse the situation; he looked across at Leon and Leon nodded. He hoped that Regan would sacrifice himself in this way.

Colleen did not move, neither did Kite, but Franky and Kate wanted nothing more than for a battle to ensue. Kate knew that, if it did, Briege would become involved herself and her revenge would be complete.

'And do you think that will stop any trouble?' Layla cried, grabbing Regan's arm. He looked at her, heartbroken, but he had no choice. If he left with Colleen he didn't care what happened to the other two vampires and Kate. They would be alone against the Highlanders, since Leon was as protective of Layla as he. He knew Kite and Franky were really cowards and would probably run at the first sign of danger.

Layla pulled him back.

'Please, Regan, don't do this. I love you,' she said.

Duncan faltered again; not only because he loved her and she didn't feel the same about him, but because he knew the pain she would feel when the American left her.

'If you leave and the others leave with you, we will spare Layla,' Ewan growled.

'No,' she shouted, 'how could you, Ewan? I thought you cared for me. We have done no one in this country or your kind any harm.'

Ewan glared at Layla. She knew perfectly well why. Some of them had already carried out terrible deeds, namely the two vampires standing with her aunt, who had orchestrated the whole thing.

Regan turned to Layla. 'Layla,' he said, 'you and I don't belong together. Every time we are someone comes to some harm and it is the right thing to do. I belong with Colleen.'

A bloody tear ran down Layla's cheek.

Ewan grunted.

'I think you should take your chances here, Regan,' Kate urged, sensing that her plan was slipping out of her control.

She'd no sooner finished her sentence than Layla pounced on her. She would destroy her, just as she had destroyed her life. Leon intervened and Kate laughed an evil shrill laugh. Duncan pulled Layla from her. Franky and Kite disappeared, just as Regan knew they would.

Regan approached Colleen. 'Help,' Layla whispered to the figure, his black attire blending him into the darkness. Was she the only one seeing him? He disappeared.

'If I leave with you, will you walk away from this?' Regan asked.

'Yes,' she said.

She had no intention of drawing any further attention to the situation.

Regan returned to Layla, but he did not speak. He simply ran his long, cool fingers over her face and wiped the other tear from her cheek.

'This is best,' he eventually whispered, 'this is who we are now and we have to live as we are supposed to. Perhaps not for our sake but for the sake of others.'

'But I'm one of you.'

He shook his head. He cupped his hands around her face and gently put his face to hers.

Duncan could not watch; he could feel the heat rising in him. He wanted to destroy the vampire, not because of his loyalty to his land but because he was so jealous that she could feel something so deep for this creature. She was still part human; he was not.

Regan let go of her face. He looked deep into her eyes. 'Go with Duncan, Layla,' he said. 'He is best for you, not I.'

Duncan's head flew up, amazed by what the vampire had just said and his calm restored.

'I love Duncan,' she said and she looked over to her Highlander friend, knowing what she was about to add would surely hurt him deeply.

'But not in that way. I love *you*, Regan with all my heart and soul, or what's left of it.'

'I know, and a truly beautiful soul it is,' he said, 'but there are others to consider.'

'He's right,' Leon said, 'you belong here. You have a human heartbeat and you will be safe with Duncan. Briege will not enter Scotland while the agreement stands as long as we all leave.'

Kate was furious but she was not strong enough to fight them all and, using their preoccupation as cover, she disappeared. It was not over for her, of that she was certain.

'What about Leon?' Layla asked.

'What about Leon?' he chimed.

'You don't belong to her,' she said, 'who do you belong to?'

'No one,' he said.

'Where will you go?'

'I'll be free to go away with Raj, anywhere I wish.'

Layla's heart was broken. Her whole world had fallen apart in front of her and she was powerless to stop it.

Regan placed his hands around her face again; he put his cold lips to hers and kissed her with wanton, hungry fervour. Duncan did not flinch; *he* would be the protector and the one she would be with; he would let the vampire have his one final kiss for Layla's sake.

Regan knew she would respond to him and he enticed her more, kissing her harder, stronger and firmer. This would be their saving grace. She could feel the trickle of blood flow down the back of her throat and finally their relationship had been consummated. She knew he was telling her it was not over. She couldn't bear to imagine him with Colleen but it was the only way they could all walk away unscathed. So she let him go.

Leon bid Regan farewell. He hugged Layla, pecked her cheek and left. Duncan put his arms around Layla giving her refuge and keeping her from chasing after the vampire. He could hear the acceleration of her heartbeat and feel her shuddering so he embraced her tighter and closer hoping he could ease the pain a little. Frazer and Ewan stepped aside. Regan walked away with Colleen. Layla's small frame quaked further, she wanted to call out after him, beg him to stay but instead she remained with Duncan as he requested. For all their sakes she fixed herself to the spot and stayed in the folds of Duncan's arms. Regan sensed every emotion Layla felt. They both gazed skyward at that precise moment, their paths were set to collide again, it was written in the stars. He did not turn, or even look, back. That time would come.